I0590771

My Home on...
Whore
Island

My Home on...
Whore
Island

DALIA LANCE

4 Horsemen
Publications, Inc.

4 Horsemen
Publications, Inc.

Published By: 4 Horsemen Publications, Inc.

4 Horsemen Publications, Inc.
PO Box 417
Sylva, NC 28779
4horsemenpublications.com
info@4horsemenpublications.com

Typesetting and Cover by Valerie Willis
Editor: Courtenay Dodds www.CourtenayDodds.com

Paperback ISBN-13: 978-1-64450-088-0
Amazon Paperback ISBN-13: 978-1-64450-002-6
Hardcover ISBN-13: 979-8-8232-0705-8
Audiobook ISBN-13: 978-1-64450-032-3
Ebook ISBN-13: 978-1-64450-001-9

DEDICATION

To those who make the juice worth the squeeze:
Burgy, Braid-my-Hair, Glitter, Rumpy, Kendy,
Wife, Stallion, Whammi, SideBitch &
My Forever Sidekick: Nobbits

ACKNOWLEDGMENTS

There are so many people I can thank in my life for encouraging me to actually achieve this goal. First my family, I am lucky to be surrounded by those who believe in me. To my friends, who are simply family from another gene-pool: You guys are always there when I need you and make my life that much more amazing because you are in it. To everyone in my life, thank you for always making me feel perfectly comfortable being me and of course loving me for it. To my writers group, the Ink Slingers Guild, I am nothing short of lucky to be surrounded by the best of the best. You make me want to be a better writer every day. To my grammar police, thank you for making sure I don't have a misplaced comma. To my editor, Courtenay, you take water and make it into wine, or in my case take trash and make it classy. Thank you for always making sure I don't fall off the path. To my publisher for simply being the one to say "I think this is a best seller", you are Amazeballs. Finally, to the two people who remind me every day that no matter what happens, the world is a pretty perfect place: Puddlebutt and my Princess Peach.

TABLE OF CONTENTS

1

It's All About Me

I think that it is best to start this story with an overview of the lead character. That would be me, Randi Michaels.

My parents thought I was going to be a boy due to a misread sonogram. I was to be named Randal after my grandfather. When I arrived with no man parts, and my parents hadn't even considered a girl name, they shortened Randal and threw an 'i' at the end.

It's important that you know first and foremost that, in present day, I am not a model. The only thing about me that resembles a model-like quality is that I am six feet tall. I have been this height since I was twelve, which leant itself to an interesting middle and high school experience.

There isn't a single thing wrong with a person being happy with who they are and how they look. I am proud of how I look and have no shame in flaunting it.

Confidence is a million times more important than appearance. If you spend your time thinking that you are not good enough, then that is how you will be perceived. So, my advice–realize that you are amazing and make sure everyone you meet knows it.

In the spirit of full disclosure, here are a few more of the details about what I see when I look in the mirror; I am well-endowed in the breast department, I have curves, and what I am told is an "Anna

Nicole Smith Ass", which one of my closest friends chooses to point out to me whenever he can.

Although I wear the same size, twelve, as she did at the peak of her modeling career, I regret to tell you that I think he was speaking of her more plump years. You have to love your friends. I know I do.

Other minor details are that I am in my early thirties, I have hazel eyes, auburn hair that falls to between my shoulder blades, and light skin with small freckles. I am not a full red head or ginger, but my Irish descent shows. Did I mention my killer smile? Not to worry, I will later.

I think it is also a good idea for you to know where it is that I came from. I did not grow up being the popular cheerleader, or whatever stereotype would make you "the cool kid" in school. In fact, I grew up a bit of an outcast. I was a bookworm. I spent most of my youth being a nerd and hiding in school libraries. Since I was always taller than all the kids in my class until I hit high school, I tended to feel awkward in most social situations.

My first boyfriend was when I was starting my freshman year of high school at age fourteen. His name was Dan (or Daniel if you asked his mother). He was taller than me, had sandy blond hair that he wore spiky, brown eyes and he was on the football team. He was a junior, and since I was a freshman that was a big deal.

It is interesting when you're younger that an age gap of a couple years is HUGE, and then in your twenties and now thirties it is more of an interesting tidbit than a defining point of a relationship.

Dan and I "went steady" for about three weeks. We never even kissed. I ended up breaking up with him when I found out that he was taking someone else to prom. Looking back, I think my decision to break up with a football player may have hurt instead of helped my high school career as far as popularity goes. Interesting that, even then, the merits you judge staying in a relationship for didn't have anything to do with the relationship itself.

Needless to say, I never ended up going to prom. On my twenty-eighth birthday I threw an 80's prom-themed birthday party. A close friend decorated her house to be the Shermer High School gym (John Hughes fans will get the reference). It was the best prom I could have asked for. I was surrounded by my best friends, *and* I knew how to get lucky with my prom date in ways I would have never imagined as a teen.

My high school career started in a tiny town in the middle of Nowhereville Wisconsin. The total population of the town was about 2,700. The school had grades Pre-K through 12th grade. I think my graduating class had about fifty people, which isn't even enough to start a good riot.

Growing up in Hollywood, California made the move to that small town horrendous. We moved there, my mother said, because she wanted me to spend more time getting to know my relatives. All I can say is that a town that doesn't even support a McDonalds is tragic.

I did make one friend during that time of adolescent torture, Beth. I met Beth because she was good friends with Missy, the unfortunate soul who was charged with showing the "new girl" around school. Since K-12 was all contained in one building, with one hallway for the high school class, I wondered what necessitated the tour guide.

Beth had ivory white skin and perfectly curly hair, which she dyed black. She wore black eyeliner and red lipstick every single day. She was the type of person who would probably look like she was sick if she didn't have her make-up on.

Beth was coolest person at the school as far as I was concerned. Of course, that wasn't the general consensus of the rest of our fifty classmates. We ended up being kindred spirits because she was also an outcast. As Beth put it one fine afternoon in detention, "I have a brain, I am sorry others regret it."

Beth was not meant for a town like that; she wasn't able to have experiences someone like her needs. After all, what kind of life experiences can you have when the only "culture" is a 4H fair and a roller rink?

This was never more apparent to me than when I returned years later. I found she was the manager of the KFC in the next small town over. Beth told me about a novel she had written. To this day I hoped to God she was able to get it published and get the hell out of that place. There are people who are cut out for the small town life. Beth and I were not "those kind" of people.

One truth that followed me throughout my freshman year was that I was most definitely a virgin in every sense of the word. Beth was not. Neither was Missy for that matter, but they never judged me for it. I would see them at parties making friends, and I just wondered when I would find Mr. Right.

As a naive freshman, I wanted that perfect movie ending to my virginity. You know the one, where you expect the boy of your dreams to appear in your life and after a little back and forth you fall madly into a Romeo & Juliet kind of love? When you finally have sex for the first time together, and it is perfect.

As an adult, you realize that Romeo & Juliet is just a short romance where six people died. This is possibly not the best goal to have.

Being in a small town, where everyone knew each other, and being a weird outsider in every sense of the word, it wasn't going to happen for me in that school or that town.

Don't get me wrong, I had crushes. I remember a guy named PJ. I was madly in love with him for a good six months. Anyone who has a crush falls into two categories: "I am sure they know and everything I do shows it", or "I just need the right moment and they will see I am the perfect person for them. I am their soul-mate." I kept hoping he would see past my dorkyness and come up to me in the library, hand me a rose and ask me to the summer dance. This of course, never happened.

The closest I ever came to a dance with him was square-dancing lessons in gym class when the teacher paired us up. My hands were sweaty and clammy, and I could not even look him in the eye. Twenty minutes of perfect torture. I am not sure why square-dancing or ballroom dancing were still in the gym curriculum, they were humiliating experiences. Ballroom dancing did come in handy later at weddings I was asked to be a bridesmaid in. I guess they did have a point after all.

2

THE MOVE

*A*t the peak of trying to fit in, we moved to Florida midway through my sophomore year. My mom thought we would have better opportunities than if we stayed in the small town. I wasn't so sure, but Tampa was a larger city and had a lot nicer weather. Did I mention I hate snow? You can be banished in Wisconsin for saying that.

Moving to Florida, I found a completely different dynamic then the small town I had just come from. Rather rapidly I began to make friends. I also found that being sixteen and a virgin was not as accepted in Tampa as it was in Nowhereville.

If you were a virgin at sixteen, it had better be a religious thing, or people assumed that something was wrong with you. In fact, I learned that it was better to have some stories, even if they were fabricated, of your sexual exploits and conquests.

In retrospect, I could have chosen better friends.

I was also starting to come out of what I consider my ugly duckling phase. I slowly began to realize people, well boys, were noticing me. It took a friend of mine, Katie, to point out to me when I was being hit on.

Being oblivious, I realized, was a gift. I was a nervous wreck when it first happened, and more so when I figured out it was happening.

Have you ever watched a movie or a TV show, and someone is completely out of their element? The 'loser' trying to be so smooth? You feel bad for the poor bastard making a fool of himself. That was me.

Yep, I think back to some of the situations where I could have been smooth and cool, and instead I ended up saying things I would hit myself for had the future version of me been standing there. Being a teenager who thinks they know it all, which every one of them seems to think they do, I wouldn't have listened. This is the sad irony of take-it-backs.

3

THE LIE

When you enter into a situation with a lie you should know right away it is going to go badly. I did just that for my first time. His name was Jacob, he was seventeen, and blue-eyed and had the most amazing smile. My friend Katie was actually dating him.

I know what you're thinking; but I only pursued him *after* they broke up. Of course it did teach me the "Never-Get-With-Your-Friend's-Ex Rule" the hard way.

In many circles I have traveled, this rule is frequently not applied. I can tell you, it is a *rule* that should be followed. If you are reading this and think that you know of a circumstance where this worked out–it was the exception. It is never worth the risk of losing friends over a hook-up. If your friend is no longer with them, there is usually a good reason. If they are the exception, you need better friends. There is always a lesson in there somewhere.

The fateful night it happened started out innocently enough. I was crashing at Jacob's house with a friend of ours, Brian. It was late, and Brian and I were too young to drive, and even if we could we also didn't have a car. Jacob's mom figured it would be safer for us to stay the night, and we could walk in the morning.

I think most parents forget what they were like when they hit puberty and the magic of hormones were injected into their system. I mean, why would you let two teenage boys sleep in the same room with a teenage girl with huge knockers? What could possibly happen?

That night, I could not fall asleep for the life of me. I was on a pile of blankets and pillows on Jacob's bedroom floor, which was tile. Jacob and Brian were on the queen bed.

Jacob's mother had insisted on the sleeping arrangements. I was sixteen, and there would be no sharing of beds with me and the boys. Of course, this is where the apparent ignorance of the parent comes into play. Since the sleeping arrangements lead to the beginning of my sex life, I suppose I shouldn't find too much fault.

I think it was about one am when I heard a noise. I felt him slide up behind me, his breath on my neck, and his arm moved around me pulling me towards him. I froze.

I must have made a noise of some kind since Jacob whispered in my ear, "Shhh you'll wake Brian."

A million things raced through my mind. One of them stood out more than any other: Jacob did not think I was a virgin.

He began kissing my neck and caressing my hips. I had no idea what to do. Part of me wanted to run from the room before I embarrassed myself. I had seen and heard what happens between boys and girls, the whole birds and bees thing. I knew that I would not be able to "walk the walk" for the "talk I had talked".

The other part of me wanted it, the same part of me that responded to his touch. He was incredibly attractive. He had one of those smiles that was slightly crooked.

I was tired of being the one that had not even been kissed for real. I started to respond to his advances. I pushed my ass up against him and moaned quietly. Guys loved to hear noise right? It was something my friend Tina had told me.

9

He responded, in fact, all of the important bits responded. He rolled me over onto my back and got on top of me. This is when I experienced one of many firsts for me over the next twenty-four hours. He kissed me. I thought I would melt. His lips felt soft, his tongue felt strong, and he was insistent. I had no choice but to follow his lead. When his tongue slid into my mouth, I wrapped mine around it. It was a dance, and I was determined to be a good partner.

Although the kissing and touching were amazing, it began to be more apparent to me that another part of him had taken a strong, firm interest in me. Just as I was about to ask what was poking me in the leg I closed my mouth. I froze again.

This was actually happening. This was really happening!

My mind began to race again. I was a virgin—a white wedding dress, halo-wearing virgin! I was pure as the driven snow. Jacob thought I had more experience than some streetwalkers thanks to the wild web of bullshit I had been weaving since moving to Tampa.

I had literally no idea what to do.

I did not want to stop. I also did not want it to hurt. I didn't want to look like an idiot. I didn't want to explain I had been lying. When you are younger, stupidly, you think the opinion of everyone around you is important enough to compromise yourself to meet expectations. I was about to give up my virginity because I was afraid of all the wrong things, mainly admitting I wasn't as cool as I had pretended I was. Stupidly, it didn't occur to me that he might actually like me for me.

You might be thinking that Jacob was taking advantage of me. He wasn't. I could have said stop and he would have. But I wanted it, I wanted him, and he knew it. Heck, I had practically thrown out a red carpet leading to my bed of pillows. I knew if he had known I was a virgin that it would not be happening that way. He would have been more gentle, he would have been more careful. He didn't know only because I hadn't been honest. The only thing I could think of was, Holy Shit!

When he moved, I thought I may have dodged a bullet for the night. Maybe I was not any good at the whole sex thing and he decided to go back to bed. It was the exact opposite. When I looked, he had pulled out a condom and was putting it on. In the faint glow of the alarm clock I saw what he was about to offer.

In hindsight, after years of experience, I can say that my approximation at that time was correct. He was HUGE, about nine inches and thick to boot.

All I could think was how much it was going to hurt and I needed to not let this happen, in this way. As he went through the motions I could not figure out a way to stop this without blurting out the truth. I was willing physically. I was *very* wet. Then he slid inside, and made the cutest moan noise ever.

POP! Extreme pain from the force of his penetration, and my cherry was gone. Then I made my noise, and I was able to say, "Stop".

I told a very confused Jacob I thought we were rushing, and if we were going to experience this moment, I did not want it to be like this. I told him I wanted to have our first time when we were not worried about waking up Brian, or having his mother walking in. I added that I wasn't sure how Katie would feel about me and him hooking up. Luckily for me, he bought it.

He kissed me deeply again, withdrew from inside me, moved back to his bed, removed the condom and went to sleep.

Jacob and I didn't work out. We never were with each other intimately again. I also never told him he was my first. Not quite the fairytale a girl hopes for, but I always say, it could have been worse.

My next experience came about six months later. It was with a cute high school wrestler named Sean. He had a bronzed body and curly black hair. Incredibly well built, with a wonderful smile and the softest lips. He took it slow with me the first time we were together. I was more honest with him, and I can say time number two was amazing. He also was the first guy to taste my "peach", if you get my meaning.

Looking back, the first few times I experienced anything sexually I ended up with all the thrill and excitement of a new experience, but at the same time I was terrified I wouldn't do something right, or I would not be as good as the person I *thought* my partner was comparing me to.

Confidence is amazing. It comes at different times for everyone. In my life, right now, that is one thing that I do not lack. I have enough for more than just me.

4

My Story

s we begin this amazing story that is about to unfold for you, I don't want you to get the wrong idea. Normally when you hear the word *whore* it is, at least per the dictionary, a person, usually a woman, who gets paid for sex.

I have never been paid for any sexual act, although, I think everyone has thought about being Julia Roberts in *Pretty Woman* at least once.

In my case, it was a fun nickname, given to me by my friends. I know what you must be thinking: *who in their right mind would let themselves be called a whore, and lovingly for that matter?*

I would.

If nothing else, I am willing to find humor in all that life holds in front of me or behind me for that matter.

The nickname came, ironically, from a discussion at my favorite coffee spot, which happens to be located inside my favorite bookstore, with four of my closest friends.

My friends are my life. They are the pieces that make me whole. They are also what makes my life entertaining, humorous, difficult, and dramatic. On that particular day, by a simple nickname, I was led to this story and a radical change to my life.

My story: How to become the Queen of Whore Island and be the envy of all your friends.

5

MY FRIENDS

It was Saturday afternoon when I decided to declare my plans. It was Alex I anticipated having either the most support or the most backlash from. Her name is actually Alexandra, sometimes reduced simply to A. She is the tallest, next to me of course, at five-foot-nine. She has milky-white skin, and dark auburn hair that is very curly. She almost always wears it straight. She hates the curls.

The "grass is always greener" is very true in the case of women and hair. Having many bad perm stories as a child and preteen, I would have literally killed for her amazingly curly hair. My hair hangs mostly straight, which means when I use a hair straightener it takes maybe five minutes. Alex hates this about me. She ends up dedicating most of an hour each night to the process of turning her curls into bone straight hair, and doesn't appreciate that I can do it with such ease.

She has dark green eyes and manages to have perfect, simple make-up all the time. She hates lipstick, but carries at least three flavors of lip-gloss.

Alex is the mean one.

Yes, that is her designation in our group. She has no hesitation telling you exactly what she is thinking. Most people, even if they say they do, do not actually want to know what you really think.

People want a version of your thoughts that coincides with theirs, thus agreeing with their views or positively reinforcing them. Alex is not the person you want to ask anything, unless you *truly* want an honest opinion.

I have a similar quality. I have a broken inner monologue button and tend to say exactly what I am thinking out loud. Most of the time what Alex is thinking is a little, if not a lot, harsher than the rest of us.

This trait was illustrated during our coffee chat when two teenage girls walked past us wearing hip-hugging jeans and those cute T-shirts that don't quite cover your stomach, showing any bellybutton decoration you might have.

One of the teen-bop sensations walking past had gemstone cherries swaying back and forth from her piercing. I think Alex's exact words were; "Would be nice if they noticed what that looks like before they left the house," and something else about "false advertising", referencing the cherries.

Both of the teen-bops were sporting very visible "tramp stamps". In case you live under a rock, a "tramp stamp" is a tattoo located on the lower back. This moniker usually refers to a female. I have seen a few tramp stamps on men; I assume the result of a bet or a night of drinking.

All four of my friends sport tattoos in the same location.

Explaining this would be pointless, as Alex had moved on to some girl standing in the diet section of the bookstore, conveniently placed outside of the coffee lounge we were seated in. The girl who, judging from her girth, had tried and failed at many diet endeavors, was about to take a sound verbal lashing from Alex.

Alex's eyes had narrowed as she honed in on her prey, when I decided to spare the poor girl and move on from people watching to more important topics. Like my sex life, or at that time, lack of.

"I don't think I want a boyfriend again," I blurted out.

Alex looked dismayed and rolled her eyes. I think she had a zinger lined up and I had just foiled it. She took another sip of her latte.

"You're just saying that," Sally replied in a comforting tone. Sally said most things in a comforting tone.

Sally is the nice one of us.

It is hard for her to find fault in anyone, much less dislike them. She is about five-foot-six, has shoulder length brown hair with coppery-red highlights, and she wears glasses. She would be the hot, nerdy, librarian type. She has the same chest size as me, and nice curves which she hides in long flowing skirts and comic book T-shirts. She tops these ensembles off with Doc Martins and big comfy button-down sweaters. Terrible sounding I know, but she always ends up driving the nerdy boys totally nuts.

"Actually, I do mean it," I said back. "I am tired of getting run over by the men I choose."

Alex gave me an approving nod followed by, "You seem to attract only stage five clingers." Grinning, she began to people watch again.

What she meant by stage five clingers was that all of my boy-friends tended to be the jobless or mostly jobless types. I would support them emotionally, financially, and defend them to any nay-sayer. When I would need help, anticipating reciprocation, I'd look around and discover they had found something else or *someone* else, better to do.

My last endeavor into boyfriendville was a waste of five years that ended with him screwing a forty-two-year-old that he worked with.

His name was Allan.

This work would be the job he had for only three weeks before the stress of having to contribute to our relationship led to him cheating. This, after he claimed to have been writing a book for nine months so he could achieve his "life goals".

He never wrote more than ten pages in that entire time. This does not a novel make. I finally told him to get a job or it was over.

He finally got a job, and of course it ended up being over.

If you have never been cheated on, I can tell you, you can't relate. I am not saying that with some loftier-than-thou attitude. Until it happened to me, I didn't know how devastating it can be on your sense of self-worth. I found myself asking questions about my value and my worth, which had no positive answers.

It turns out there is a void of questions that no answers could fill. Instead, I decided that I wouldn't put myself in that position ever again. I think most people tend to wall themselves off from getting hurt again, especially when the wound is fresh.

At times, I wonder why I am not just a tad more bitter and depressed, but then I remember that Alex is bitter for me.

Ignoring Alex's comment, Sally said, "You just need to find your Mr. Right."

Lucy, having been quiet the entire time, finally nodded and said, "Yes, your prince charming."

I looked up from my coffee long enough to glare at both of them. They just smiled back. Bitches!

It is hard to be to mean to either one of them. Lucy is the emotional one of our group. I call her the emo one. I stole that from modern, hip-kid lingo. She wears her heart on her sleeve. The newest to our group, she fit in immediately. She is also the most fashionable, with long, straight, jet-black hair and dark brown eyes that glisten gold in the light, she looks like she just stepped off a runway.

Lucy works as a spa director. If you catch her on a bad day, she will tell you she is an over-glorified receptionist. She is actually the manager and a trained aesthetician. This means she gets all of the perks of the spa for almost nothing, and has a professional vantage point for all things beauty. Needless to say, even in comfy clothes, she makes the rest of us look like rejects from a sale rack at Walmart.

I just sighed.

Thank God Baley walked over from grabbing some bakery treats for all of us to share. "Randi just needs a little play time," she said.

I nodded in agreement, "That is exactly what I need."

Baley is the flirty one. She is the one who we can count on to be cute at a moment's notice. She is the same height as Sally, but with a fuller frame. She keeps her hair very straight and *very* red. She is tanned, and has amazingly bright blue eyes.

As Baley set the plate and plastic forks down, Alex finally looked back towards the table, and grabbing a bite of the molten chocolate goodness that had been provided said, "I think she should forgo the dating thing and just have a lot of good sex."

And as simple as that, it began.

When you are not sure what you are doing that attracts all the wrong kind of person, you have to take a step back and figure out what about you needs to change. That would be the smart thing to do. Instead, I decided not to look. I wasn't ready to deal with it. I wanted to see if a completely different path would suit me better.

Sally and Lucy desperately wanted to protest the whole thing, but I think even they had to admit something had to change. I needed to have some fun, and that was something everyone could agree on.

6

I'm a Pilot, I can Fly

My first encounter as a newly liberated whore was interesting. It did not have the same tone as any following it, which I am incredibly happy to report. Going into the evening, I was not expecting it to end the way it did. If I had known the ending, then the adventure would have been a lot less impressive.

I love to go out dancing, and most times I drag my friends with me. That particular night we decided to go to a retro club called Bricktown 54.

Bricktown plays dance hits from the 70's, 80's, and 90's with a few modern hits sprinkled in. The club is quite large, and has an oversized lava lamp and Rubik's Cube spinning in the center of two of the four bar areas. It has posters from dance movies plastering the walls, everything from *Grease* to *Purple Rain*. The amazing atmosphere notwithstanding, we loved it because it played all the songs we loved shaking our asses to.

The club mainly catered to an older crowd as well. You had to be at least twenty-three to get in the door. This meant Bricktown didn't have the usual "I just turned twenty-one, so I am going to party 'til I puke" type of people. The age limits made the crowd a totally mixed bag. You could have a cute old couple dancing together or a middle-aged guy with a mullet hitting on a girl with mall bangs and a snakeskin miniskirt. Then there are those patrons, like us, who come to dance without being in a club so packed you end up grinding on those dancing next to you because there isn't any room.

This night it was Alex, Baley, Sally and me. We're regulars. I am not sure what that says about us, but it's great because the doorman doesn't even ask for our IDs anymore.

When we arrived, I scanned the crowd. The club was more crowded than usual. This was a good thing. There were a total of four levels, two off the main floor, a third one wrapped around the entire club, filled with booths and tables. The fourth level was VIP. Since we never forked over money for the elusive membership to enter that sacred space, I knew our dignity was still intact.

We made our way up to the second level because that was where our favorite bartenders usually worked. They tended to hook us up drink-wise, and they were really nice to look at. As we approached the bar, my favorite eye candy looked up and smiled.

As a rule, I don't think one should have sex with a person you want an advantage from in social situations such as those. What if you or he doesn't enjoy the encounter? If you don't, you have to pretend that you did, and if asked to repeat the experience you would have to be slick as hell to avoid being forced to endure it again and still maintain your "in" with them. If for some reason he didn't enjoy it, you are completely screwed in the perks department. If you leave it be, and just flirt, then there is always that tension there. That way, it's possible to end up with a lot more than spreading your legs will get you.

You can refer to that as *"Whore Tip"*.

Because I have gained what I hope is wisdom throughout my adventures in "Whoreville", I will do my best to impart these gems in the hope of guiding you away from unnecessary mistakes. You're welcome.

Whore Tip: Never sleep with the help. 😊

This hot bartender was about as tall as me, with black hair and green eyes. "Good evening ladies, what can I get you," he said as he leaned over the bar. I leaned over the bar as well, making sure my assets were positioned perfectly, and put my head next to his so I could whisper into his ear. There was, of course, no need to get that close, except for my own personal gratification. I did my best sexy voice as I tried to whisper in the noisy club. I gave him our drink order; he smiled and then winked and went about getting it ready for us.

I looked over at Alex and Baley, who were both texting on their phones. Alex cannot live without her cell phone. Sally was looking out at the dance floor, and I began to scan the crowd.

I don't want it to seem like we were on the prowl, far from it. As I stated before, I love to dance, and so does Sally. Alex and Baley were more there to get their drink on, and once they do, they are totally up for shaking their booty.

As the sexy bartender handed us our Cherry Bomb shots (a vicious drink which consists of cherry vodka and an energy drink), we left a big tip and headed to a table.

> *Whore Tip: Never drink more than three of these in a night. Know your limits. There is cute drunk and there is idiot drunk. Please make sure you know the difference.*

We always chose a table next to the dance floor. This allowed us to stay close to each other when we were dancing, and if one of us got in trouble we could do the "big eye" gesture for help.

What is the 'big-eye' gesture? This is when a friend in need, trapped by some hideous yuck of a man, looks over at you and opens her eyes really wide as if screaming, "Dear God, help me before I have to kill myself to get away from this loser!" Look around a club sometime; check out any two girls talking to guys they don't want to. You will see it.

Whore Tip: Learn to use the "big eye" gesture. Teach your friends. It is a subtle lifesaver.

After the ceremonial Cherry Bomb was ingested, Sally and I went to dance. I was wearing jeans, sandals with a small heel, and an emerald-green top that was sleeveless and plunged in the front. Sally and I danced for a couple of songs, and then Alex waved at me. Round two of the Cherry Bombs were ready.

As we exited the floor, I felt a hand on my right arm. I looked over and I met one of the lightest pairs of blue eyes I have ever seen. He had short-cut blond hair, lighter skin, an angular face and a great smile. He used that smile and said, "I'm going to buy you a drink."

Normally, I would totally blow off a guy in that situation. First, I was out with my friends; second, you never date someone you meet in a bar. Other than a naughty dance or two, I don't like to give dance partners false hopes.

Yet he stood a tad taller than me, had wide shoulders, and looked completely yummy. I decided to take the plunge.

I leaned into him, placed one hand on his chest and told him, "Rum and coke, and I will be waiting when you get back." He smiled and I felt his hand leave my arm, and my hand slide from his chest.

He made his way to the bar, and I quickly ran over to the girls. I downed the drink that was waiting and, as quickly as I could, told my friends a recap of my recent interaction. Alex laughed, and made some joke about how I must emit some kind of pheromone, because I never seemed to have a problem attracting men.

This is true, no ego included. The problem was the type of men I attracted. It was not the time to point this out.

Before long, I saw him heading back with drink in hand, and I moved back over to the spot where he had left me.

You have to keep in mind, I can flirt and do all the cute girly things, and I am not saying that I had never had a sexual encounter that didn't have a repeat; I just hadn't had an actual one night stand.

I had never picked someone up, and I was a little nervous, though the drinks were helping with that.

We met where we had started and he said, "Thought you had ditched me for a minute."

I smiled as I took the drink and replied, "Not with those eyes," taking a sip.

"I was watching you out there. I love the way you move."

I bit my lower lip a little.

Trust me; I know this was a bit cheesy, but in my experience, that's almost everything any guy has at that stage of the game—cheesy lines they hope will be the right thing to say.

It is all in the delivery. I was not trying to find Mr. Right; I was more interested in finding Mr. Right Now. For me, it is all about if their "moves" hit the bar I set for them. That bar is completely arbitrary, and has moved several times since I set it originally.

We talked for a few minutes and I discovered his name was Sean. He was a pilot for the local sheriff's department, and flew helicopters.

After a bit, he asked about my friends. I motioned them over and introduced each one, Alex being the last. He asked what we all did, as in jobs. Alex was quick to answer that we were all strippers that did some movies. His face lit up like a kid in a candy store. Don't get me wrong, most guys would find four strippers who did porn to be a treat.

Most people are smart enough to really know the difference between fantasy and reality. We did not look like stripper porn stars and Sean, we could all tell, was dumb. The fact that he was cute was the only reason the conversation continued.

Sean ended up buying all of us and himself, many drinks. I have to mention that Sally doesn't drink. She has an alcohol allergy, and therefore gets the distinct advantage in these situations of being sober for the entire thing. Also, lucky for the rest of us, she is always the designated driver. You should never go anywhere without one.

We danced more, and chatted more. The talking of course led to me putting him in the category of men who is better seen than heard. As two am rolled around we, the girls and I, were ready to go, but like a puppy playing with a new toy Sean followed me out. He asked if he could show me his truck. He had just gotten a new stereo and was really proud of it.

This is where this encounter begins to take on the telltale signs of a bad high school date.

I told him that I would be delighted to see his new stereo. If that was what he wanted, maybe I could get a little of what *I* wanted.

Once in the truck, all bets were off. He grabbed me and pulled me close to him. He started kissing me franticly. His mouth felt like it was engulfing the entire lower half of my face. Yep, I thought, just like the boys in high school.

I finally pushed him away gently. He tasted like beer. I figured that the bad kissing was quite possibly a side effect of being drunk, and I did not want to judge too harshly. I mean, after all, those eyes and that body deserved a chance.

He put his hand on my leg just above my knee; I could feel his warm hand through my jeans. I leaned into him again, this time controlling the kiss.

My lips played gently against his, as my tongue gently caressed his lips and then slid it into his mouth, making sure I was ready to accept his into mine. I did not let him take control at any point for fear he might take over my face again. His hand moved up my thigh just as Alex tapped on the window.

I looked up to see her face with a little smirk on it and nodded. She walked away and I asked, "Would you like to continue this some other time?"

He said yes before I could even finish the question. I asked for his cell phone number. I typed it in, and sent him a text while in the car: "This is Randi, call me sometime to play."

Enough drinks and I had become a pro at this.

When I heard his phone go off with the text, I gave him one last kiss and slid out of his truck with his hand trailing all the way down my leg.

I got in Sally's car, and the girls wanted all the details. I, of course, told them everything. Alex said, "And it begins with a Pilot."

Sally laughed and Baley asked, "What begins?"

"Randi's vacation to Whore Island," Alex replied.

That was the beginning and I knew it.

7

I'M THUMPING, THAT'S WHY THEY CALL ME...

The next week actually went by pretty uneventfully. The Pilot did not call. I did not worry about it much. Of course, there was that small part of me that wondered why he hadn't called, but when I started having the "Oh my god, why hasn't he called?" shakes, I gave myself a reality check. It doesn't work to have "no strings attached" if you attach strings.

Instead, I chalked it up to a drunken mini-tryst. For the first time in my history of relationships and dating, I was able to categorize the experience for exactly what it was; making out after a night of drinking and dancing. There was no commitment, no required call, no obligatory waiting to see if he was really interested. It was liberating.

Ladies (and gentlemen for that matter), the above is another reason why picking up people in bars can be dangerous. A make-out session, groping, or a one night stand is really all you can expect out of it. I am not saying that a full relationship cannot develop, what I am saying is: that is the exception and not the rule. Most of the time, I find people wake up the next day and chalk up anything they did the night before to being drunk, instead of poor choices. If you are going to make the choice, let the drinks be the lubricant instead of the justifier.

The following Friday night, I was on the phone with Alex deciding what to do for the evening. Her fiancé was out of town and the great debate was whether to go dancing or pour ourselves into comfy clothes and go watch a movie. The drawback to the movie was that teenagers tended to invade—yes *invade*—theaters on Friday and Saturday nights. I do not have tremendous patience for this when I want to have a cinematic experience with popcorn included.

As I was looking into what was playing, the phone beeped and I didn't recognize the number. I told Alex to hold and clicked over.

"Hello?" I said, in the voice willing to hang up in a moment's notice if it was a telemarketer.

A male voice asked, "Is this Randi?"

Pausing only for a minute I replied, "Yep, who is this?" It was the Pilot.

> *Whore Tip: Always save numbers in your phone with a name or note to remind you who it is. You never want to be caught off guard.*

He asked if I wanted to go with him and a friend to a local bar and have a drink. He was heading out and had thought of me. I was tempted to ask what that thought was, but I didn't. I asked him to hold and clicked over to Alex. "You up for an adventure?" I asked. I told her what the Pilot said, and explained that I did not want to go alone. Since it was the first time I was meeting someone I had only really met while I had drinks in me, I wanted backup, just in case it turned out to be a bad idea. She said okay and I could pick her up in thirty minutes. I clicked back over and I told the Pilot I would be there in about an hour.

I got ready by throwing on, tight jeans, a low cut top and simple make-up. I threw my hair up in a clip and grabbed my ID card, cash and keys. I have a rule when I go out almost everywhere. I don't believe in purses, especially in clubs. All you need should fit in your pockets. I hate seeing girls on the dance floor clinging to their little purses, or sometimes ridiculously large purses. It just looks stupid. This rule applies to bars, concerts—almost any activity that involves crowds.

Not long after leaving my place, I pulled up at Alex's house. I texted her I was outside. Yes, we are like that. If we have the technology, we should use it. If God wanted me to walk out in the heat of a hot Florida night, he would not have given me a cell phone.

She arrived wearing a similar outfit to mine, jeans and a cotton T-shirt. Her hair was up in a clip. She hadn't straightened it, indicating she was simply going as friend support. I thanked her again and we headed over.

We pulled up to the bar, a place called Dazzles. When he told me the name, I knew exactly where it was. With a name like Dazzles, the first thing you think is a bar for alternative lifestyles, but it's just a small sports bar in a strip-mall shopping center. I had never been inside, but the name grabs you. I guess that is the point.

I didn't see his truck in the parking lot. One night of making out in a truck, when you're drunk, doesn't make you an expert on someone though. We headed inside.

I wasn't ready for the inside of this delightful establishment. Most bars or restaurants in strip malls have one entrance, but take up at least two or more of the shops in a row. This had only one. There was a small bar along the left wall with about ten stools, and two twenty-inch TV screens showing different sports channels. To the right of the bar was a single, worn out pool table, a jukebox, and three round tables with two chairs each. There were a total of eight people in the whole bar, including Alex and me.

I think I would have been willing to leave at that point if Sean hadn't spotted me, not a hard feat, and waved us over. Alex squeezed my arm as we approached the table Sean and his friend were sitting at. Sean was wearing jeans and a button-down shirt. He looked more sober than the earlier night, but you could tell he had started without us. His friend looked literally like a toad. He had no neck, and a flabby face that was rounder on the bottom then the top. His eyes were kind of buggy and he was wearing jeans, a button up top and a sports jacket. He also had a very curly mullet.

Alex's grip on my arm was painful. She was not having this, not even for a minute. The Toad offered to buy us drinks. He had a name, but for the life of me it was gone the second he said it. I ordered a rum and coke. It would be polite to have one drink before we made an excuse to leave.

When he asked Alex, she simply shook her head no and kept her arms crossed. Alex stared at me with her eyes just a little too wide. She was doing "big eyes" even though I was right there.

The Toad headed off to get the drink. All I could think was that I must be a little braver. I mean, alcohol is what they use to sterilize stuff, right? I sighed. I knew that this would have to be over sooner than waiting for the drink to return. Alex wasn't interested in any sort of small talk with the amphibian. This meant that if I wanted to get The Pilot alone, I couldn't unleash the Kraken that was an angry Alex on The Toad.

I explained to The Pilot, after The Toad was out of earshot, that Alex actually couldn't stay. That she got called from work on our way over and we had to leave, but I hadn't wanted to stand him up. He made the pouty face it seems all guys are trained to make. I said I could have the one drink, but we had to jet quickly.

He was quick with the solution. He wanted to spend more time with me that night, so he would finish up with The Toad, (he didn't call him that but, again, the name was gone once said), call me, and we could maybe watch a movie at his house. I smiled. I was going to get lucky, and that was what I wanted.

The Toad came back, the most sickening smile on his face, directed at Alex, and handed me the drink. I chugged it down in one gulp, put the glass down, winked at The Pilot and said, "Thanks." I turned and walked out. No explanation at all.

We got in the car and Alex said what we were both thinking. "That guy looked like a character from a George Lucas movie." We both laughed and I took her home.

> *Whore Tip: Never stay in a situation to make someone you hardly know happy or comfortable when you are not. Always be willing to walk away.*

I got home and about thirty minutes later the Pilot called. He gave me directions to his house and I headed over. His house was a nice yellow with white trim. Before I was able to knock on the door, he opened it and let me in. He gave me a little tour, and it was a cute place.

I could tell you all about the décor and the furniture, but that is not why you are reading my story. I will skip to the last room, which was his bedroom.

As he was giving me the tour, telling me about different things in his house, it became even more apparent that he was not very smart, witty or funny. I wasn't there for the conversation. I treated the conversation the same way I do when it is something I'm are not interested in listening to. I watch for facial queues or tone changes and do a lot of nodding.

Facing the bedroom from the doorway, I did the obligatory scan of the room and said, "It's really nice." It consisted of a queen-size bed, a dresser with a mirror, a nightstand with a lamp, and it was boring.

Just as I started to wonder if I had made a bad choice, he came up behind me, put his hands around my waist, and began to kiss my neck and shoulders. I let myself lean into him and moved my hips to press myself up against him. With his next kiss, I moaned slightly and that was all he needed. The right noise is all most men need as incentive. He turned me to face him and kissed me.

I began to think I was in school again. He couldn't kiss without almost inhaling the lower half of my face. It was almost like the middle school boys you got stuck with during "Spin the Bottle" or "7 Minutes of Heaven". When you're younger, you don't know better and think it is messy. As an adult, it can be gross.

Since I was there, and it was my first encounter since the big break-up, I decided to not judge too harshly and hoped The Pilot had some other skills.

I finally backed away from him, since no matter the angle I moved my head, it had the same result: slobbery.

Whore Tip: If at first you don't succeed in kissing try, try again. If it is still terrible in round two–TAP OUT!

I decided to push the limits to get to the good stuff. I pulled my shirt off while sliding off my shoes. I knew if I let the make out session continue, I wouldn't want to do anything more. On some level I had to talk myself into what I was doing. I had never shown up on a guy's doorstep with the sole intention of getting laid.

He pulled off his shirt, and I was happy to see that he did have a nice body. He was lean, and had almost no hair on his chest. What little he did have was the same color blond as the hair on his head. He looked at me and smiled again. Looking into those pale blue eyes I remembered why I was there. I undid my jeans and slid them down until I could take them off with just my feet.

He slid his jeans off as well, until he was just wearing his boxers. I could see that he was ready for me. His very hard cock was pressed against the fabric, creating a tent-like effect. My favorite male underwear is boxer briefs. They hold a guy, erect or not, in place. I used to think I enjoyed boxers, but I like being able to see exactly what I'm working with more.

He walked the distance between us and put his hands on my waist. I thought he wanted to go in for another round of kissing. Instead, I began to move backward, letting him maintain his hold, and hopefully guiding me to the bed.

I felt the bed against the back of my legs and he continued forward until our bodies were against each other. I could feel his hardness pressed against me.

He leaned in to kiss me, again, so I let myself fall back. It was quite sly. He didn't see it as avoiding him, and instead took it as a sign of eagerness. He slid off his boxers and let me see all of him. He was well hung; my guess was seven inches and nicely cylindrical. He leaned over me and pulled my panties off, kissing down my stomach and legs as he did.

He stood, opened the drawer of his nightstand and pulled out a condom.

I had brought a "Just-In-Case" case with me. I shall explain this magical item. It is a small make-up bag you should always have on you if you are in the market for playmates. It should contain a few condoms of different sizes, a small container of lubricant, some moist towelettes, and of course some mints or gum. These are all the items you should need on a quick night out with a friend.

> *Whore Tip: Always keep a Just-in-Case case. It is a whore's best friend.*

He slid the condom over his cock and then pulled me to him, so my ass was on the edge of the bed and my legs were spread open for him. He leaned onto me and guided himself inside.

Although the foreplay was brief, because of my insistence that the kissing had to end, I was wet and ready for him. Looking back, I think it was his interest and desire for me that was biggest turn-on, coupled with how naughty I felt for even doing it.

Then it happened. It wasn't even slow at first. It was instantaneous. The Pilot was humping me like a rabbit. I know you hear girls say that, but that is exactly what happened.

They were exactly measured thrusts, in and out, no change, no finesse-just speed. He simply pounded me. I had been in that situation before when I was younger, having sex as a teenage girl with teenage boys who were not sure what they were supposed to do. However, that had ended years ago, and now I felt like I was in a sexual time warp.

I am not sure how long I spent feeling like I was being attacked by Thumper. He stopped rather suddenly and asked me to flip over onto my knees. I was at a loss, should I just get up and walk out? I didn't. I instead got on my knees and hoped it would get better. It didn't.

He slid in again and asked me, "You like this baby?"

I needed to end this, so I tried to help it along. "Yeah baby, make me cum hard," I replied.

I was the one who started the fling, so I felt it only fair to see it through. You can never say that I'm not a trooper. You know, taking one for the team. Sigh.

He began humping me again, as I began my best impression of a porn star: moaning louder and throwing in a couple of "Oh baby's" and "Yes, yes, yes's". Within moments, he climaxed. From the smug smile on his face, he thought I did as well.

I lay on the bed for a moment and debated what the next step I should take would be. He propped himself up on one arm on the bed and asked me, "How was that?"

I smiled as I stood, put my jeans and shirt back on, slid on my shoes and wadded my panties in my hand. I turned to look into those gorgeous blue eyes and said, "It was something."

He was grinning when I walked out. "Have a great night," he called after me. What an idiot.

As much as I would like to blame The Pilot for the horrible encounter, I had to acknowledge that I had stayed. I knew the moment I kissed him that it was going to crash into a fiery ball, but I tried it anyhow. I didn't owe him anything, because I had no investment other than my time.

You should never stay when you are not having a good time. It was good to have popped my "Whore Cherry", but I knew I wouldn't settle again. Never compromise.

8

Houston, We Have a Problem

I called Alex when I left and told her the whole thing. She couldn't stop laughing. For the next few days, she emailed me every picture of a rabbit she could find, even texting me daily with, "I'm thumping, that's why they call me Thumper." Did I mention she is the mean one?

The Pilot tried calling me the next day to see if I wanted to go out. I told him I was very busy for the next week. I did not hear from him for a month, so I thought he caught on.

Out of the blue he called me one night and asked if I was up for a party with him and a friend, you know, The Toad. He told me he couldn't get over the amazing night we had together and thought that I might be up for some more adventure, hopefully willing to be shared with his friend. I just hung up the phone.

About a week later, Alex, Baley and I were driving to a club when we saw The Pilot walking down the side of the road. We pulled over and he looked at us with no recognition at all. He was drunk and gave us a story about having his car keys taken by a friend when he was leaving a bar. He asked us if we were up for a party. Alex said yes. I smirked as he got into the car and we drove.

He talked the whole way about the party he thought we were going to. Alex told him our names were Mary, Sherry and Cherry. At one point, he looked at me and said he knew me from somewhere. Alex chimed in that maybe it was from high school. He seemed puzzled.

When we finally arrived at the party destination and he got out of the car, it was fun to see the shock and surprise on his face that he was looking at his own house. He turned to say something but we were already driving away.

The ending to the Pilot was as climactic as the sex was, at least for me. He called several more times, but I never took the call. Eventually, like any show on Animal Planet, I would like to think he found his true mate, as most animals do. A cute bunny for Thumper.

WANT TO GO SHOPPING?

W e are on the "Information Super-Highway."

I hate that term by the way.

With the advent of online dating/hook-up sites, it has suddenly made it ridiculously easy to meet people. It has also made it incredibly easy to meet a bunch of freaky weirdos as well.

I was not one of the first to jump on this bandwagon.

I hate that term, too.

Baley is the queen of making profiles. She came over one night, after months of harping on me, and set up my very first profile page.

She told me it was a great way to hook up with friends from the past. I did find many friends I had not spoken to in years. I also found an even better use. Shopping for fun! Okay fine, that might sound terribly slutty, but if that is what you are looking for, the internet is where you can find it. I'm not ashamed to say it can be one of my favorite places to shop.

After about a week my page was basically complete. Photos, 'About Me', and way too many questions about my favorite every-things were all filled out. I was set.

Keeping track, which I was told to do, I had even acquired about fifteen friends. Woohoo, go me! I was smoking. I did not completely understand all the possibilities until a Friday night when I received an email which said:

Subject: Hi =)

Your profile pics are hot. Are you into younger guys?

I clicked on his page to find a twenty-year-old guy. His page was full of pictures of his car, his friends and of course, the obligatory photo array of him with his shirt off.

I was stunned that this guy was trolling for someone over the age of eighteen, but there he was. I mean who are we kidding? I'm not even close to a cougar, but it's sort of hot in a Mrs. Robinson kind of way.

Don't believe for a second that I didn't know that younger guys can be into older women. I mean, there was an entire movie about it. I just didn't realize how prevalent it was online. If I was shopping, they were hunting.

Of course, I emailed him back:

Yes.

I know; it could have been more poetic. I could have even used a whole sentence, but poetry was not what I was looking for.

When he emailed me back the next day, I found out his name was Chris and he wanted to meet me. That was one of the four other emails I received that day basically asking the same thing. I was forming a list of very willing twenty-something's.

> *Whore Tip: Learn to shop. You will find the selection is good, and you never want to buy the first thing you see. Make sure there isn't something else that fits better.*

I realized that a foray into younger men could be fun and a lot less likely to come with entanglements.

When I showed Sally and Alex the emails, they did not understand what it was about me, or this age of website wonder, that was causing the onslaught of potential play toys. They got emails on their profiles, but for the most part they were from creepy old guys or the occasional hottie that instantly turned stalker.

Sally simply stated, "I am going to live vicariously through you."

Although Chris didn't work out, mainly because he seemed a little too clingy in the first couple of emails, I did discover that shopping for men, especially younger men, was very easy indeed.

> *Whore Tip: Never let your age define you, unless that is what <u>you</u> want to be defined by. You will find there is no age gap between horny consenting adults.*

10

Brief Intermission

O n dating sites, all of the conversations start with a very similar email that usually leads to a text chat online. It will usually be a compliment or two and then a question that will open the door for me to reply. Never reply to anyone who doesn't have the brains to at least try and engage in conversation.

Also, as a note of advice in these circumstances, you always want to attempt to weed out the weirdo stalkers before meeting them in person. There are red flags and you need to be aware of them.

The top three are:

1.) They only "like" the same things you like. It might appear as if you have a ton in common, you don't. This means they don't know who they are, and are looking for someone to give themselves an identity.

2.) Tells you about a horrible ex right off the bat. This is bad. You are not supposed to air your dirty laundry. This is also a tactic to get you to feel sorry for them. Don't. There are two sides to every story, and you're only hearing one–from a relative stranger.

3.) They start talking about sex right out of the gate. I know you might think I am contradicting myself. They are simply trolling. I know. They will tell you everything you want to hear, and even seem like you are the only one who had inspired this in them. You're not.

Whore Tip: Make sure you test the waters before taking the plunge in any online situation. Regardless if it is a one-time thing or a several time thing, the person you are talking to is a total stranger. Treat them that way.

I talked to about eight guys before I met Richard. He was nineteen, about six foot two inches tall, lean but muscled, blond hair cut short with blue eyes.

The first thing that grabbed me was that he looked like Justin Timberlake. He was not an exact replica, but it was a bit uncanny. And seriously ladies, how many of you have Mr. Timberlake on your list of five? (To clarify: The "list of five" is a reference to the list of five movie/music stars you can sleep with, even if you're in a relationship. Of course both parties have to agree to this rule.)

He emailed:

Subject: WOW!!!!

I wanted to stop by and say how amazingly beautiful your pictures are. Hit me up sometime if you would like to chat.

I responded:

I would love to chat.

Yes, this is how it works, that simple. The stories all show a long string of conversation, being coy, cute or even witty. But if you are looking to simply rip each other's clothes off, you don't need to have it be something pretty, just true.

He responded right away and we chatted for about an hour. It shocked me; he was very funny and charming.

More shocking was that we had something to talk about for an hour.

During the conversation, I made sure I was very clear about what I was looking for, or more specifically, what I wasn't. He was in perfect agreement, which made me like him even more. He asked me what I was doing the next night. I told him I did not have any plans. He asked me if I wanted to go to a movie. I said that sounded great and gave him directions to pick me up.

> *Whore Tip: Don't talk about details of your life or theirs. Get the basics, but the better you know them, the more likely they will begin to believe you are something other than "friends with benefits".*

I called Sally and told her the whole story. "You're just going to let this guy pick you up," she said, a little stunned.

"Yes?" was all I could say. She didn't feel I was being completely safe, and she may have been right. To ease her anxiety over the obviously dangerous situation I was in, I provided her the following information: the link to his profile page, his online name, his real name and his phone number.

I told her she could text me and I would let her know I was okay.

Even if I felt she was overreacting, I knew it was safer to agree and simply provide information on each playmate. This became a pattern with her. Whenever I was out with someone, she had all the info I had. In case something happened, she could start the police on the trail to find my body. I know it sounds grizzly, but again, these people you are meeting are strangers and you only know what they are telling you.

Whore Tip: Always ensure you have a safety net in place. Even if it's writing down all the information on a piece of paper and sticking it to your fridge. If you turn up missing it will be a place to start.

I got ready for Richard to pick me up at seven. I decided to wear jeans, a tight-fitting v-neck T-shirt, half-sweater and flip-flops. My hair was pulled up into a clip with little tendrils at the sides and natural looking makeup. This was all topped with glittery raspberry gloss.

He pulled up in a silver convertible. He had sunglasses, slightly baggy jeans and a button-down dress shirt. I was not disappointed.

I opened the door and a huge smile came across his face.

"Hi," I said, returning the smile.

As he walked up to my door I said, "I must say it is *nice* to meet you."

This caused him to chuckle a little. You would be amazed how well people respond when you are honest with them and say what you are really thinking.

He reached out his hand and I took it. He raised it to his lips and kissed it. "It is *very nice* to meet you too," he replied. For a nineteen year old, he was smooth, in a good way.

We walked to the car and he opened the door for me. Being a gentleman is never a bad thing. I am all for women having power, but it is sometimes very nice to be treated as something prized.

As we began driving to the movies he kept looking over and smiling. I would look over, not staring, but I couldn't help but notice how pleased he either seemed with me or himself. I finally turned and asked what he was smiling about.

"You're even more gorgeous then your pictures, and you have an amazing smile," he responded, looking directly into my eyes.

"I have to say, you're pretty amazing yourself," I said.

We chatted on our way to the movies, but the tension was already there. I knew the moment I had opened my front door that I had to have him.

We got to the movies and he let me choose what I wanted to see. No, we did not decide beforehand. I looked online and there were a lot of movies that started around seven-thirty pm, so I knew we would find something. I settled on a comedy. I don't remember the name or what it was about. I suppose it could be a key part of the story, but it wasn't.

Richard asked if I wanted anything from the snack bar. I didn't. "I'm good," is all I replied, with a little smirk. My thoughts were that what I wanted wasn't going to be satisfied by a snack bar. This I kept to myself. I let him choose the seats. He chose ones near the back in the middle. The theater ended up having about eight more patrons total, and they spread out so that we had plenty of seats between us and them.

We chatted before the previews started. I found that Richard was a waiter. He had been working at Chili's since high school. He wanted to get into real estate and was planning on going to college for a business degree. He told me that he was actually very surprised I agreed to go out with him. He had just gotten out of a year-long relationship and did not want anything too heavy. That worked for me.

I told him again that I was not looking for anything more than a friend with benefits. This was the first time I had said this to a guy out loud. I think he had asked me again to make sure what we discussed online was real and that I wasn't going to turn all clingy.

Whore Tip: Always be honest about what you want. Leading a person on or getting in deeper than you want will only end badly.

He seemed very excited by the prospect of a completely sexual arrangement. As the movie began, he whispered in my ear, "I hope I can give you what you want."

A little grin played across my lips and I whispered back, "I hope so too."

The movie was torture. Both of us were trying to behave ourselves. He reached down and put his hand on my thigh at one point and it made me shiver. The tension was unbelievable. I know we both felt it. If something started in the theater, it would also need to finish there.

> *Whore Tip: Public sexual acts can lead to being arrested. This is a huge turn-off in case you were wondering.*

As the credits rolled he stood up and grabbing my hand, he playfully pulled me up against him. Although we had been sitting very close before, I was now touching his body. He looked into my eyes and slid his arm around my waist, his mouth hovering so close to mine.

Looking directly into his eyes, I was holding my breath and then it happened. My eyes closed as my breath released and his lips touched mine. A moan escaped my lips as he pulled me closer and my tongue met his as we tasted each other. His lips were soft and strong.

He wanted me and I could feel it in every area that touched me. I moved my free arm, sliding it around his shoulders, fingertips sliding into his hair. I felt him tense for a moment and then release.

I pulled back from him, still leaving my hand in his. He reached for me and before we were violating the theater seats, I whispered against his lips, "Not here." He smiled and like a kid with a new toy who wants to hurry home and play with it, turned and led me out of the theater and back to the car.

We didn't say much on the way back to my house. When we arrived at the house and I walked up and unlocked the door, he was right behind me. I could feel his breath on my neck. As we walked in, I set my keys down on the stand right inside the door and turned around to face him.

In a moment his arms slid around me and pushed me against the wall. He used his foot to push the door closed. My hands ran up his chest to his face and pulled his lips to mine. The kiss was fierce. I could not get enough of him. I let my tongue trace the outside of his lips, and then I leaned so I could kiss the line of his jaw and down his neck. It was his turn to make noises. As my lips kissed and my tongue continued to taste him, he whispered, "God, your amazing, Randi."

I think every person loves to hear their name during sex. I am no exception. I started to unbutton his shirt and slid it off his arms. He was wearing a white undershirt which I made disappear just as quickly.

As his arms came down from the removal of clothing, I moved towards the bedroom and he followed. I cast aside the sweater I had been wearing as we entered the doorway and he grabbed the edges of my shirt and pulled it off.

He discarded it on the floor and pulled at the button of my jeans, sliding them down to my feet. I stepped out of them. His hands slid all the way up my legs, gently touching my skin as he looked up into my eyes. He was gorgeous.

I would love to say that I was used to this, or it happened all the time. That was far from the truth. I stood there hoping that I was the sex goddess he wanted, while my stomach was doing cartwheels.

When he stood again he lifted me off the floor and put me on the bed, then slid up on top of me.

He kissed my lips gently and said, "Randi, I need to tell you something." I opened my mouth to speak and he laid his finger on my lips to silence me. "Please let me finish while I still can." He suddenly seemed nervous. "I have never done anything like this before." I had to bite my lip not to say something and let him continue.

"I have only ever been with girls from high school, only three actually. I want to please you." He sighed a little and looked down at my face, caressing my cheek with his fingers. "I am asking you to tell me what you want me to do."

This made me smile.

I traced his lips with my fingertip and then kissed him gently. He was blushing. I realized that no matter how different this was for me, I had the upper hand. I had the experience to know what I wanted.

"I promise to teach you exactly how to please me, but you're already off to an amazing start," I said back and winked.

> *Whore Tip: Be willing to always share with your partner. Most people love to please, and this is usually a bigger turn on than being pleased.*

He smiled and leaned in again, kissing my lips, and then moved down to my neck and shoulders. His hands explored, and I let him. Like any new toy, he wanted to feel every part of it.

I worked my hands down to remove his jeans, that were still on and in my way. Undoing the belt, unzipping them and sliding them down to his hips, I was able to wrap one of my legs around him. Hooking my foot into the fabric, I pushed the jeans down and pulled myself against him at the same time.

He was hard as a rock.

I slid my hand back up the outside of the fabric of his boxers as his jeans hit the floor. His swollen cock moved against my hand. Through the slit in the front of the boxers, I felt up to the tip where there was a little wet spot. I glided a circle around the head of him with my fingertips and his back arched as he moaned.

I pulled my hands back and playfully licked my upper lip. He smiled back and moved so he was kneeling between my legs, his hands cupping my breasts on the outside of my bra. His mouth went to my erect nipples. Taking them through the fabric, he gently bit with his teeth. This time my back arched.

He used this opportunity to slide his hands around to undo my bra. As he pulled it off, holding my breasts in his hands he mouthed, "Wow." He bent down to them again, his mouth covering one nipple, tasting it, rolling it around with his tongue, as his fingers tugged at the other. Back and forth he went until he brought my nipples together, tasting them both at the same time.

I am not quiet in bed. Some girls describe themselves as a screamer. This would be an accurate statement in my case.

As his mouth gently kissed and licked his way down my stomach my legs spread wider. He kissed down my thigh to my knee on each side. For a brief moment the thought crossed my mind that he was way too good to be as new to this as he claimed. Then his fingertips played the lips between my legs and I forgot everything I was thinking as my hands grabbed the blanket beneath me.

His tongue slid up the entire length of my outer lips before he forced it between them. His hands cupped under my ass and he pulled me to his mouth. Although the initial feeling of him tasting me was amazing, it became very apparent that he had very little idea what he was doing in this department.

I would give him an 'A' for effort.

Since I needed a little more than effort to cum, I needed to change the music, so to speak.

I moaned one more time very loudly. (So I faked that one, don't judge me.) Then, in a breathy voice I moaned, "I need you inside me." That always works. (Again, don't judge me.)

He climbed up on top of me, sliding off his boxers. He was ready, and I mean rock-hard ready. I reached over to the nightstand and opened the top drawer to pull out a condom. I removed one and handed it to him.

I threw the others on top of the stand as he knelt and slid the one I gave him on and tossed aside the wrapper.

I moved so I was kneeling in front of him, almost touching. He looked at me with a questioning look, and I leaned in and kissed him. Gently biting his lower lip, I said, "Trust me."

I pushed him down on the bed, placed my legs so I was straddling him and slid his now condom-clad cock inside of me. Admittedly, I have a bit of skill in this department.

I do realize this might add to my apparent sluttiness, but the skill of being able to please yourself sexually is important.

As I slid down the length of his shaft, about seven inches for those keeping track; his hands went to my hips. I leaned down on all fours then, and rocked up and down, tilting my hips and grinding against him. With my clit brushing against him with each stroke, I could feel myself tightening around his cock.

I felt my orgasm building; my moans were growing louder, as were his. He was close. Very close.

His hands reached up to cup my breasts and his fingers wrapped around my nipples and tugged. That was all I needed. I pushed myself down on him as my back arched and I came hard. With perfect timing he grabbed my waist and thrust himself even deeper inside with his orgasm. I felt him dig his fingers into me, as if afraid any motion would be too much to handle.

I lay on top of him. Each of us trying to catch our breath, as his fingertips made little trails on my back, sending shivers through me and causing mini-spasms which caused small noises to escape from him.

He spoke first.

Clearing his throat he said, "That was amazing." I met his gaze then, with a little smirk on my face. I winked and rolled off of him, stretching out my legs.

After a few minutes of staring at the ceiling fan, he rolled onto his side to face me. "I mean that, Randi," he said, as if trying to ensure his words held weight.

Did I mention that I love it when they say my name?

"I know that some people just say the words to make the other person feel good. This... was the best sex I have ever had," he said. I looked at him for a second longer and then he touched my face and said, in almost a pleading tone, "Please believe me."

I held his gaze, and without looking away said, "I do believe you, Richard." I figured since he used my name it was only fair to use his. I know; I am terrible.

The amazing thing about younger guys, generally speaking, is they are able to recharge their batteries more quickly. Richard and I enjoyed each other once more before I told him that I had to get up in the morning. He was sweet as he left, promising me to call for another play date soon.

I learned to trust my confidence more during this encounter. I know that it is easy to be critical of yourself, your own judge and jury, but you have to remember to take a moment to see yourself through the other person's eyes. Richard thought I was amazing. I chose to agree with him.

11

Bringing Sexy Back

While Richard was an interesting toy to play with, I found it even more fun to talk about him with the girls. The retelling of my adventures, and sometimes misadventures, made for good stories for my friends.

Richard was fun because he was so young, and it was rare not to have someone his age come with the usual teenage stuff. In my thirties, what I was looking for in a relationship, before my trip to Whore Island, was not the same as what I was looking for in my teens or twenties.

Giving each of my playmates nicknames made it easier to remember who they were. When I hit my third Eric, I was thankful for the bright idea. So Richard or Rich became: Brief Intermission or BI for short.

I called him that because he would come over whenever I asked him, and leave whenever I told him, AKA brief intermissions in my life.

I ended up playing with BI for many months; he was my first regular playmate. Since it lasted more than a couple of times, the girls got curious and wanted to meet him.

I had explained that he looked like Justin Timberlake, so I was surprised it took them as long as it did to make the request. One night, I arranged a meeting.

Sally was at my house with her boyfriend, conveniently leaving, as BI was showing up. He arrived and Sally and I made it seem like an accident. When I opened the door to invite him in, I made the introductions, which was a little awkward since I accidentally introduced him as BI. Sally acted as if she knew nothing and he was simply a friend she hadn't met yet. Later, he told me he thought it was funny since he had known about the nickname, and liked it.

"Oh my, silly me, I thought she would be gone before you arrived," I told him after they left. He bought it. I didn't think I could keep repeating the accidental run-ins, but I would figure something out if the other girls insisted on meeting him after Sally's report.

It wasn't long after Sally left that she texted me. She told me I was right, he looked exactly like Justin Timberlake, and she was incredibly jealous. This made me smile. I told BI what she said.

He sang *Bringing Sexy Back* when he was inside me that night. That was something to check off the Bucket List.

Other than the sneaky meeting of the friends, being honest with BI about everything simply made things easier. He would text or call, or I would, to see if the other was free. Sometimes we had other things, or people, to do. That didn't matter. We were able to have amazing sex, and yes, he was a quick learner, any time we got together without any obligations. It helped to break me of any lingering neediness. When both parties are synced on the exact nature of the relationship, life is smooth sailing.

12

"Are You Going to Take Those Socks Off?"

After BI, I wasn't done shopping. Although I could have kept the one, and did whenever I wanted, my goal was to play. If you are only playing with one other person it is not very challenging and doesn't really warrant a trip to Whore Island.

Like BI, I met Todd on a dating site. Todd was an artist. He was a painter by trade and was making a fairly good living at it. He mainly did abstracts and had posted several pictures of his work on his profile page. A starving artist can be hot, but the non-starving kinds are even hotter.

When I first saw his picture, I wasn't completely sure why he was emailing me. He looked like a typical jock, totally built and tanned, with dirty-blond hair that seemed in that perfectly perpetual messy stage. He was over six feet tall and had the most beautiful blue eyes I've ever seen in my life.

He had several pictures, of course, where he was not wearing a shirt. The fact that he looked appetizing would be an understatement. He also had pictures wearing a button-down shirt with jeans, which may possibly be one of the yummiest looks a man can have.

> *Whore Tip: Never doubt your attractiveness to*
> *someone who is interested in you, and never be sur-*
> *prised that you drive them wild. Everyone's bell is*
> *wrung by a different kind of gong.*

In the spirit of not wanting to look a gift horse in the mouth, I spoke with him back-and-forth by email for about a week, and eventually we exchanged numbers. The interesting part was he was one of the few guys that didn't want to meet up front. He told me he wanted to hear my voice and wanted to listen to what I sounded like when I talked about certain subjects. I never had given thought as to whether I had a seductive voice, but I was up for new experiences, and I figured that it was about time I found out.

We ended up talking on the phone almost every day for about two weeks. We learned a lot about each other's desires. He was surprised that I meant what I said about no strings. He didn't think that it was possible for a girl. "I guess I am just full of surprises," I told him once. He was telling me, again, that what I was offering was so *surprising* to him.

When I asked why he hadn't been snapped up by a head cheerleader somewhere, he laughed and told me he had just gotten out of a bad relationship with a woman with whom he had a child.

He told me that they were never married and they had stayed together for over a year after the birth, to see if they could make it work for the sake of the child. They were not a good fit he told me. I didn't ask any more about it. I didn't want to know and he didn't insist on telling me either.

That information was going into the "getting to know them on a personal level", which is what you do when you date. This wasn't dating.

A lot of our conversations were about how we would do this "playing" with each other. Both of our schedules were quite crazy, and it seemed that meeting at my place one day after work might be the best way to meet up.

Todd had a lot of fantasies he wanted fulfilled. Most guys have fantasies, but what I found when I began playing is that most men have not been with the type of woman who is willing to fulfill those fantasies. Most men are too nervous to ask, for fear they will be rebuked.

> *Whore Tip: Being someone's fantasy is the easiest way to end up with what you want most. If you are willing to be what they want, most partners are more than happy to reciprocate.*

Fantasies for women usually involve a specific location or items, such as rose petals, or a bubble bath. For men, their fantasies likely include positions and costumes. Some even want role-playing.

In Todd's case, he was easy to please. His fantasy was having a schoolgirl. This is a fantasy for most males, and one you can fulfill over and over again. You just need the outfit. A cute white button-down shirt with short sleeves, a red patterned miniskirt with pleats, black penny loafers, and knee-high white socks. Don't forget the matching red lace bra and boy shorts. Interestingly enough, most guys don't want a thong with this particular outfit as the look is naughty enough on its own. Top the whole thing off with pigtails or a ponytail, and natural looking make-up.

They really want innocence in the encounter.

Todd told me one day via text that he would be available the following Wednesday and was hoping I was as well. Of course I had to check my schedule, but amazingly enough I was able to free myself up. I would have blown off my own birthday to meet him that Wednesday, but you never want to come off as too easy, and he would never know that.

Whore Tip: There is a VERY fine line between eager and desperate. Don't cross this line if you want to keep your playmate.

I told Alex about it. She thought it was possible that he was too good to be true, that he wouldn't look like his picture, and instead a four-hundred-pound troll of a man with boils on his face would be on my doorstep and there would be nothing I could do about it.

I laughed when she said it, but I was suddenly terrified at the thought of standing there, all made up with my cute smile and then, BAM! I would be scrambling to send away the monster that showed up at my door.

I was so worried, I called Sally later that night and had her look up his page. She was totally into this trip to Whoreville of mine, and said Todd was incredibly cute. She wanted all the details after I met him. I didn't tell her what Alex said.

I took what Sally said, and pushed Alex's thoughts away. Not because Alex wasn't right. She could have been. I pushed them away because it was not what I wanted to hear. I know, very adult of me, huh?

Whore Tip: Trust yourself, always.

With much anticipation, Wednesday finally arrived. It was a terrible work day, because I could not concentrate or get anything worthwhile accomplished. All I could think about were blue eyes staring up at me from between my legs.

I raced home right after work. The way we had set up the meeting, I didn't have a lot of time to get ready. I jumped in the shower within moments of hitting the door and got ready in record time. I had texted Sally all the details, since not following her rule was not worth the scolding, and part of me was afraid she would show up during the act. That is not something you recover from, almost as bad as mom walking in.

Todd was supposed to arrive at six pm. The doorbell rang at five-forty-nine pm. I waited a couple of breaths before answering because I was nervous, and didn't want to flip into the desperate category.

I liked letting anticipation build up. I began to find the butterflies in my stomach almost soothing. They had started to mean something amazing was coming. Hopefully that something would be me.

I opened the door. He was looking out from the porch and turned back. His eyes met mine, and I was immediately lost in those pools of blue. They were intense not only in color, but their need, as he drank me in.

He looked me up and down more than once. "Wow." I backed up to allow him in. He seemed almost frozen, which made me smile. It is not often you get that type of response.

He followed me in, his eyes never stopping their probing. The hunger I had heard in his voice so many times on the phone was in full force now. Small talk was not going to happen. I had no idea what to say. Time seemed to stand still, and I had to fight to just remember to breathe. This was something I had never experienced before: pure lust.

I guided him to the bedroom by slow steps and movements. I twirled my skirt a little, licked my lips, and slowly bit my lower lip as if I was innocent and unsure what to do next. This was what he wanted. This was his fantasy, and I could see I was fulfilling it by the look on his face.

When we got into the bedroom, I turned my back on him and walked towards the bed slowly. If I was the innocent schoolgirl, I wasn't going to make the first move. I don't know if it was the moment or the desire I could see in every look he gave me, but my confidence was astounding, even to me. I had this.

When he came up behind me and I could feel his breath on my neck, I shivered. His fingers gently caressed each shoulder and down my arms. He was savoring it, the feel of me. His hands found my waist and he gently turned me to face him.

I didn't meet his gaze at first, playing shy and timid. I was so good at this it was scary, and he loved every second of it.

He placed his fingers under my chin and raised my face to meet his gaze. I bit my lip again. That was all he needed. His lips pushed against mine with such ferocity it was as if I had just let out a caged animal.

I felt his tongue thrust between my lips, tasting, drinking me in. He was not gentle and I responded perfectly. His lips left mine as he knelt down in front of me. He removed my shoes, and then moved up under my skirt to remove my panties. His fingers undid every button on my shirt, and slid it off. He stepped back to admire his handiwork.

I stood clad only in my red lace bra, skirt and knee-high socks. He gestured for me to spin around. I smiled, and clasped my hands behind me and slowly spun in a circle. His smile told me he was more than pleased. He was unbuttoning his shirt and sliding off his shoes as I completed my circle. His jeans were next. He wasn't wearing any underclothes besides his socks, and he was more than ready for me.

Grabbing me by the waist, he thrust his tongue inside my mouth again. His hands felt hot, and I melted as I felt his rock hard member throb against me. He spun me around so he was pressed against my backside. His hands moved up to cup my breasts and he kissed and nibbled up my shoulders to my neck, finally reaching my ear. He whispered in a husky voice, "Can I have anything I want?"

My reply was so faint, I wasn't even sure that it was out loud. "Yes."

He squeezed tighter, almost kneading my breasts. He guided me to the edge of the bed and pushed me forward so that I had to kneel on the bed or fall. I knew exactly what he wanted and I wanted it more.

I knelt on the bed and so that I was perfectly lined up in front of him. I heard him make a growling noise. His hands lifted my skirt, and I felt his lips against my skin. Holding me firmly in place, his tongue began the probe between my legs.

My hands grabbed the blankets as my back arched. It took all the willpower I could muster to hold myself still. All he wanted was to please me. He wanted to make me scream. I felt his lips and tongue taste all of me. My core was swollen and throbbing, I climaxed within moments of his devouring me.

It wasn't enough for him. He needed more, and it didn't take long for him to bring me to orgasm again. The moans escaping my lips were driving his need. I felt him move. I heard the wrapper, and then felt him thrust himself inside me, deep and hard.

I could tell that whatever restraint, if any, he may have had was gone. There was nothing but his hunger left, and he was going to take what he wanted.

He thrust deeper and harder with every stroke. As he grew inside of me, I could feel my wetness tighten around him. It was perfect symmetry. I felt him begin to climax, and this brought me again. When he exploded, his grip on me was almost paralyzing.

After we disengaged, I lay down, my legs shaking uncontrollably. I knew I couldn't hold myself up, let alone catch my breath. He lay down next to me, moving tendrils of my hair out of my face and smiling. I smiled back.

Nothing needed to be said. I could not have imagined a more perfect moment. I looked down the length of his gorgeous frame and noticed that his socks were still on. It grabbed my attention as somehow out of place. Why the hell would he leave just his socks on? I understood mine; it was part of the outfit. I could even understand leaving panties on during sex, but men's white sport socks? There is nothing at all sexy about that.

It wasn't long before we needed to part ways. I think the only words we spoke as he left were him thanking me for "a perfect moment in time" as he put it, and me saying to call me next time he needed help with his homework.

I was proud of that. How many times in life do you get to say the exact right line at the exact right moment? Almost never. I looked forward to seeing what his next fantasy was.

13

FILLING THE SOCK DRAWER

I called Sally right away and told her every detail. She told me I had better share with the group. It was a perfect story for Penthouse, she thought. The next night the girls and I met at the usual coffee spot and, over some yummy cheesecake, I relayed the night with Todd. I left out the part about the socks being left on. I didn't want to ruin the image for anyone else.

Alex and Sally were happy for me. My friend Sarah, who has over thirty-two tattoos, most of which are visible, wanted his number.

Whore Tip: Never share with your friends. It can get very messy, and not in a good way.

Baley and Lucy were less than amused. They thought I might have been too reckless. I didn't even have to answer the scolding because Alex jumped in and told them both to stop being such prissy bitches and be happy I was having so much fun. It is at those times that I truly love Alex.

Over the course of the next week, Todd and I discussed our next meeting. Next on his fantasy list was me wearing a men's button-down white collared shirt and nothing else. It made me think a little of the movie Risky Business, and, of course, I was game. If the encounter would be anything like the last time, I was absolutely in.

It seemed to work out to pick another weeknight. Again he arrived a few minutes early, and this time we didn't even make it to the bedroom before it began.

This time, I was able remove every piece of his clothing and push him down on to the couch. He was rock hard as I leaned in, and I started by kissing and licking down the entire length of him until I was able to slide the tip of him in my mouth.

He almost jumped and grabbed the couch.

I slid my mouth all the way down his shaft, letting my tongue wrap around with each stroke. It didn't take long before he told me to stop; he was close and wanted to explode inside of me.

I slid a condom on his shaft and mounted him. His hands grabbed the shirt and pulled it over my head. His fingers held my breasts, then grabbed my nipples and tugged me to him. I moved my hips up and down faster, as our tongues entwined. I couldn't get enough of him.

I began to moan and, as I came, I felt him explode.

After we finished, we were lying with each other on the couch in a mess of clothes and couch pillows when his phone went off. It was laying on the floor, having fallen out of his pocket in our hasty removal of clothing.

And yes, he still had his socks on. I picked up his phone and handed it to him. It was a woman, by the picture of the smiling blond on his phone. I didn't care about the call, we had no rules, but his entire demeanor changed. He bolted off the couch and said he had to take the call.

He walked into the bathroom as I grabbed my shirt, the only piece of clothing I had at hand, and put it back on. I began to straighten up the room, and could hear the discussion he was having get very heated. Because he was behind closed doors and I wasn't going to be nosy, I didn't try to make out the words, but when he came out of the bathroom he seemed flustered.

"Everything Okay?" I asked. I knew it wasn't.

He sighed and said, "I have to go." He put on his clothes that I had gathered into a pile during the call.

Part of me wanted to ask him who was on the phone and what had gotten him so upset, but that would violate the rules–no personal stuff. So I kept my mouth closed and he left.

He didn't call or text for a few days. I didn't take it personally. No strings.

When he finally reached out, he asked me what I was up to. I told him I was reading, which was true. He asked me if I was able to take off time during the day from work. I asked him, "Why?" He told me that he really couldn't come by at night anymore. Red Flag. Again, I asked, "Why?"

This is when his previous story fell apart.

He wasn't married, but he *was* engaged. No, they were not broken up. He just didn't know if she was what he wanted. They had met and in the beginning months of their relationship she became pregnant. Now she was about to give birth and he didn't know what he should do. This sucked, I thought. He had been fun.

Whore Tip: When there are red flags, find the lie and walk away.

He had broken more than one of the rules of the type of relationship we had agreed to. Besides being far into the realm of too much personal information, he was not single. He also wore his socks the second time we were together. That should have tipped me off.

I did the only thing I could. I told him that I would be arranging my sock drawer for a while and I would let him know when I would be available. He thought I was joking, but after not responding to any calls or texts for a few weeks, I think he got the hint.

Whore Tip: NEVER be with someone who isn't single. Regardless of their reason for wanting to play, it is a

*terrible thing to do to their other half, because you
never know when* you *might be that other half.*

As much fun as Todd was, I never want to be the other woman.
I knew what it felt like to be betrayed. Part of me wanted to find
his woman and tell her everything, but sometimes it's better to just
walk away. My experience with Todd dragged me back a little and
propelled me forward at the same time.

14

RED SOX

*Y*es, to answer the obvious question, the next foray into the unknown was with a Red Sox fan.

We met online and his name was Eric. He was my first Eric, if you are going to keep track.

He was Italian and from some northern state. He was twenty-seven, and worked as a sales manager. I didn't really care if I knew his profession, but it was listed on his page.

When we began chatting, I let him know early on what I was looking for. By his reaction he didn't really believe me. This was a pattern: men couldn't believe a girl would just want a playmate; they kept waiting for some other imagined shoe to drop. In this case, I was happy to disappoint.

Since he was hard to convince of my intentions I let him ask me questions. It ended up being the same question, just asked different ways to see if my answer would change.

He asked me, "So you're not seeing anyone?"

When I answered that I wasn't in a relationship with anyone, I think he thought I was being evasive.

Truthfully, I was still having BI over every now and then to play. He was getting a lot better. You would be amazed what a little practice can do.

The next question was a little blunter: "Are you having sex with anyone?"

I was honest. "Yes, I am."

I wasn't sure if he didn't know what to think of me or if I was some mysterious creature men only dreamed existed. I would like to think it was the latter. His urgency to meet me picked up after that, proving I was right.

Our schedules were not really compatible over the next week, unless I could meet him later in the evening. I had no problem with that and told him I would love to pop over.

Again, Sally was set up with all the information on Eric. After the lectures from the girls the last time, I decided that meeting at my house wasn't the safest idea. Looking back on it, going to a strangers' houses for sex doesn't seem that brilliant either. That is what experiences teach us I suppose; how to not be such a dumbass.

It was a Thursday evening around nine pm and I headed over to his apartment. It was easy enough to find the apartment complex, not so easy to find his building. It was a very warm evening and I wore shorts, a tank top and flip-flops, with my hair up.

I don't want you to get the idea that after four partners, I was getting lazy. I assure you, I wasn't. It was just hot! Until you have suffered through a Florida summer, you have no idea what hot really means.

My outfit was cute, and I had on light eyeliner, mascara and glitter gloss. It is never good when the humidity melts the make-up off your face.

> *Whore Tip: Never overdo it. Be yourself and dress so that you are comfortable, unless of course you're in costume. You can suffer a little for that.*

I called him, unable to find his place. Directing me to his apartment, we chatted until I got to his door. This didn't allow for any nervousness to sink in. He was standing in the doorway as I walked up, and when I saw him I became an instant Red Sox fan.

He was a couple inches taller than me, with jet-black hair that was cropped. He had olive skin and very angular features, and was wearing a white T-shirt and blue gym shorts that hit just above his knees. He lived on the second floor and was smiling as I walked up the stairs. I slid my phone and keys in my pocket.

He motioned me in as he held the door.

I walked in and I could tell I was definitely in a bachelor pad. He had a huge TV that covered almost an entire wall of his living room, and of course there was a game on. His couch was U-shaped and took up most of the floor space, with a square coffee table in the middle that held several remotes.

He closed the door and asked me if I wanted anything to drink. I told him I didn't and he began to walk past me, and then stopped. He turned, still smiling, and before I realized what was happening he had his arms around me and his lips were pressing into mine. Gentle at first and then he was squeezing me into him as his kiss became more urgent. His tongue pushed between my lips and I let him lead me.

A first kiss can go from bad to terrible if you are not careful how you approach it.

> *Whore Tip: Always let the person who started the kiss lead. Otherwise you will step on each other's tongues, so to speak.*

As his lips disengaged from mine, his grip did not lessen. He looked into my eyes. "I wanted to do that the moment I saw you," he breathed, and began to kiss me again.

My arms slid up his until my fingertips were pushing through his hair, pulling him closer to me. A small moan escaped my lips as he kissed me deeper, his tongue probing. He tasted like orange candy. I pulled back a little and ran my tongue over his lips slowly.

As the kissing continued, he began leading me away from the living room. I could only assume that we were heading to the bedroom because my back was to our destination. He was careful not to run me into anything, but my flip-flops were lost in the process. Apparently they were not meant to go backwards.

I stopped only when the back of my legs met the edge of the bed and he lowered me down. He never released his grip and he never stopped the kiss. I was very impressed.

When I was on my back, he finally pulled back and rested on his arms on each side of my head. He looked down, still smiling. "Am I going too fast?" he asked.

I looked at him for a moment. His eyes were such a dark brown they looked almost black. It is moments like this where you realize how much power you have. The smile at the corners of his mouth began to lessen and I could tell he was losing his confidence in the situation. I smiled back at him, licked my lips and said in husky whisper, "I am wondering why you stopped." His smile lit up again, even brighter.

He kissed me again, but began to kiss down my neck, nibbling lightly enough to send shivers through me but not hard enough to leave a mark.

> *Whore Tip: Never get a hickey where anyone can see it. We are not in middle school. It simply looks trashy, no matter how great it might have felt receiving it.*

He kissed down my shoulder as he straddled me and pulled my tank top over my head. He left my bra on and kissed down my chest, using his teeth on the outside of the fabric where my nipples were. He bit down just enough and my back arched slightly. My hands moved up his sides to his back, pulling him to me. I could feel the muscles under his shirt. He had told me he went to the gym every day before work, and I believed him.

He moved down, using his tongue to trace his path. He moved off the bed and removed his shirt with a quick motion. I slowly lowered my gaze from his face down his body, taking it all in. He was very well built. His chest was firm with the perfect amount of black curly hair. My eyes traveled, following the slight amount of hair, down his six-pack abs to the lines of his hips.

Those hip lines are my favorite. If a guy is well sculpted, wearing pants or in this case gym shorts, that sit right at that line, it is heaven.

I looked back up and met his gaze; I realized he had been doing the same assessment of me. He knelt down at the edge of the bed and undid the button and zipper of my shorts, pulling them off.

His lips were on my skin again, picking up right where he left off, his tongue tracing the edge of my cotton panties that were becoming quite wet. My back arched again and his fingertips slid down my hips, hooking the sides of my panties and pulling them down past my feet.

He slowly spread my legs apart, exploring up each thigh with his mouth. I could feel his warm breath against my skin. "Tell me how much you want it," he said.

Eric had told me when we spoke that his fantasy involved being with a girl who was willing to be naughty. He found most girls were not confident enough in themselves or comfortable enough in the bedroom to say what they really wanted.

I, of course, did not suffer from such ailments.

I raised my head again and met his gaze. "Please baby, give it to me," I breathed. "I need it, I need you."

I had never really talked dirty in bed, not because I was opposed to it, I just hadn't been asked to do it and it wasn't my natural inclination. I *have* always been vocal. "Oh, God" and "Yes!" and "Oh, Baby" were normally what came from my lips between moans. I was willing to say whatever he wanted to hear for him to continue.

His mouth pressed into me, his tongue drinking me in. He wrapped his arm around my thighs and pulled me to him. Tasting me, he was gentle at first and then faster. My hands grabbed the sheets as my back arched. It took only a few moments for moans to escape my lips, and I screamed, "More! I am so close, baby, make me cum for you," as my legs began to quiver. He sucked on my swollen clit and I climaxed.

He released his grip on me and stood up. He stripped off his shorts and I could see he was ready for me–very ready for me.

> *Whore Tip: Penis size only matters in relation to your "cash-and-prizes". There is a too-small and a too-big, but filling you the way you want to be filled is all that counts. Judge length and girth in relation to getting you off, not in relation to other partners.*

I could tell Eric would be a good fit. He was above-average length and the tip had a little bend to the left.

I sat up and took him in my hand. I gently kissed his stomach, stroking him softly. With encounters such as these, you can totally tease a guy without appearing to tease. The trick is to go at a much slower speed than you know he wants to go, while being sensual and sexual the whole time. This will work him up even more, and can absolutely be to your advantage. Unless, of course, you desire slow and romantic, then make sure you haven't pushed him into fourth gear.

After a couple of minutes of me tracing my lips and tongue around his erect cock, Eric pulled me up to a standing position. His grasp was aggressive, but I liked knowing that the need he was feeling was caused by me.

He spun us around so his back was to the bed. With a grin on my lips, I pushed him back on the bed. I moved around to the foot of the bed and he turned, matching my position. I don't take my eyes from his; I wanted to look at his entire body lying in front of me. The smirk on his lips, and the way he was watching me were intoxicating. "I want to ride you until I explode," I said in a low, seductive tone.

He grabbed a condom off the nightstand, slid it on and did a little head nod. "You want this, baby?" he asked. He put his hands under his head as if he didn't have a care in the world.

I crawled up the bed on top of him and straddled his hips, allowing his very hard member to slide between my lips. "I want all of it," I said. He placed his hands on my legs, moving them up slowly. I felt him throb as my hips tilted forward and backward.

When his hands reached my hips, he pulled me to him. I leaned down and kissed him deeply; lifting my hips, I was able to slide him in deeper. I sat up quickly, and then thrust myself down, hard and deep. A moan escaped his lips as his fingertips dug into me, holding on for life.

"You make me so wet," I said as I start to move, placing my hands on either side of his shoulders. I rode him, moving faster, and his hips begin to lift to meet my pace.

Moans escaped me as the friction of rubbing my clit against him brought me to climax. My back arched as my spasms squeezed all around his throbbing cock.

As I recovered, I began to slow. I looked down to meet the incredible need in his gaze. He was close, and he was letting me have total control. It was an amazing feeling.

I leaned close to his ear and whispered, "I want to feel you explode inside me," and moved faster, again pushing him deeper.

Grabbing my hips and pulling me to him, I felt his explosion inside me. After his release, he let his hands fall from my hips as he gave into the moment. His eyes closed and he looked euphoric. I sat atop him, felt his throbs inside of me and knew I had been amazing. You gain so much confidence when you are able to step back and admire your handiwork.

Lying next to him recovering, I decided that it would be best not to stay the night. It would give the wrong impression, plus I had work the next morning. I did not attempt to cuddle and fall asleep, instead I got off of him and the bed, got dressed, leaned down to kiss him and said, "Sweet dreams."

I think he was a bit shocked when I headed out of the bedroom, grabbed my flip-flops and moved down the stairs towards my car.

He called about the time I was pulling out of his complex.

"Heya sexy, miss me already?" I said as I answered the phone. I could tell that I threw him off a bit. He regained his composure and told me that I hadn't needed to leave, I could have stayed.

I told him that I knew I could have stayed. I explained that both of us needed to work in the morning and I was sure that we would play together again soon.

This made him laugh a little and tell me, "You are possibly the most amazing woman I have ever met."

I replied, "I am."

We agreed to chat the next day and I drove the rest of the way home proud of my show of confidence throughout the evening.

I had started down my journey only a few months before and I found that my confidence continued to expand. Not because I thought I was better than anyone else. I just knew what I was capable of. I had gained a tremendous amount of confidence in my ability to please my partners. This caused a level of happiness in an area of my life I hadn't known was lacking.

15

STRIKE ONE,
TWO & THREE

Eric texted at about nine am the next day to say good morning. I asked if he had slept well. He said he had, and really wanted to see me again. I replied I would like that very much, but I was going out of town with friends that weekend and we would have to meet up after that.

He texted me several times a day, asking all kinds of questions, mainly about my sexual desires, fantasies, what had I done, and with whom I had done it. He was turned on by the thought of me being with other men.

He really did want a girl that would be with him _and_ other men. He didn't even have to know them, in fact he preferred if they were complete strangers. Eric simply required that his girl come over and have sex with him, give all the details about her encounter, right after the sex she had with the other men. It gave a whole new meaning to sloppy seconds.

Although I considered myself adventurous, I wasn't sure a relationship, especially one of that nature, was something I needed or wanted.

Eric was persistent and seemed smitten.

Our schedules, however, did not seem as smitten with each other, and for a couple weeks we couldn't seem to find a time to meet up again. Finally, we were able to nail down a night we would both be free and we set a time to meet up for dinner and some drinks. Of course, it should lead to the second inning (I realize the baseball puns are terrible, but just go with it).

It was Friday and the end of an absolutely crazy week for me at work. When I finally had a moment, I checked my phone and noticed that I hadn't gotten a text from Eric. That was odd, considering the frequency he had been texting since the first night.

I texted him: "Hope your day is good, looking forward to tonight."

He didn't text back.

When I got home around six, I began to get a funny feeling that something was up, but I had made it a firm policy not to read into situations.

Whore Tip: Reading into any kind of situation only does one thing: it makes you "that girl".

I decided the fastest approach to end my wondering would be to call, which I did. It rang until I got his voicemail. I left a quick message, and decided to not get ready until I heard from him. I didn't hear from him until almost three days later, on Monday morning.

He texted: "Hey gorgeous. How was your weekend?"

The situation had so many different directions that it could head in. I could get mad, I could be upset—which has a little bit of mad and sad mixed together, I could be sad, or I could be accusatory. Instead I opted for: "Good. Yours?"

I found out through the next few days of texting that he wasn't going to say anything about blowing me off. He behaved as if it never happened.

I wasn't sure exactly why I continued talking with him. I wasn't invested at all, but as Alex kept pointing out, it was like some sort of horrible relationship car wreck that I just couldn't seem to walk away from.

After another week of "We should meet up again" texts, he failed to keep our date for a second time. I was done.

> *Whore Tip: Letting someone lead you on is nothing but idiocy. If they want you, then they'll make the time. If they don't, regardless of the words coming out of their mouths, their actions tell a whole different story.*

He stopped texting after the second time failure to show, and I filed him under the "do not repeat" category in my phone.

It takes three strikes in baseball, and that was just strike one.

Strike two came some time later. I had all but forgotten about Eric, when about two years later I got a random text that said: "Hey, is this Randi?"

I, of course, had him listed in my phone as "Red Sox – Don't".

> *Whore Tip: Never, and I mean NEVER delete a number from a good or bad date. You don't know when they will try to slide back into your life, and it is better to see it coming, sometimes a warning, as to what to expect.*

I coyly replied: "Yes, why, who is this?"

"This is Eric, remember me?"

My reply; "How could I forget?" could have been taken a couple of different ways, but I think sarcasm is hard to do via text.

He asked me what I was up to and if I wanted to hang out again sometime.

I typed: "Honestly, you were basically an asshole, so no, not really," and hit Send. In case you hadn't realized by now, I believe in honesty.

After about twenty apologies he explained that it had been a rough time in his life. His grandmother had been very sick and eventually passed away. He had been a wreck, and felt terrible about what he had done. He summed it up with; "If you never want to speak to me I understand. But even though it is years after we met, I still can't get you out of my head."

Well crap! Dead grandmother and it had been two years. What was I supposed to do? Talk to my friends about it.

I talked it over with Alex and Sally before I responded to the last text. Alex said I should ignore him, and Sally said I should give him a shot. With those two in particular, when it comes to matters of the heart, ninety percent of the time I get different answers from them on what to do. On some level, that is why I asked them. I should have just called Baley; she would have been on team hookup.

Regardless of the good advice I was given by Alex, that I should have paid attention to, I told him I would give him another shot.

He seemed excited about my willingness to not blow him off the map. So, we started texting again. He loved to ask questions and most I didn't mind answering. He was still looking for a girl who wanted to sleep with other guys. I am sure there is judgment occurring when reading those words, but the idea was intriguing.

Unfortunately, when we finally met up for dinner, the first thing he said was, "I almost didn't make it tonight because I don't feel good."

It seemed the sweet, sexy, romantic guy I had been speaking to had been replaced by a whiny, sickly and complaining person.

It was one of the worst dinners I ever sat though. When we parted, we both did the obligatory "look forward to seeing you again soon" statements, but neither of us meant it.

I didn't hear from Eric again. I know I've only listed two strikes. Strike three was, and was not Eric. Read on and I'll explain.

I received an email about six months after the last time I had spoken to Eric, from a person who said we had met on a dating website a couple years previously. He wondered if I remembered him. (I didn't.) He said we had only spoken briefly and that he had been speaking with me and another girl, they met before we had the chance, and started dating. He was now single and thought of me first.

I was flattered, but I still didn't remember him. His said his name was Travis and he sent me a couple of pictures. He was cute and we emailed back and forth for a day. He was witty, funny and we seemed to share a lot of similar interests. He asked if we could meet up and go to dinner that week. I told him that sounded great, but I had one condition: that we speak on the phone. He agreed and said he would call me in a bit, that he was at work.

Whore Tip: Trust your gut. When things feel a little weird, make sure you know that your instincts are spot on.

About an hour later, I was in my laundry room and I received a text message from Eric that said, "Hey, who is this?"

I responded with, "This is Randi, who is this?"

He replied, "This is Travis; sorry I got your number confused."

This is reason number two that I always save phone numbers. Eric was saved in my phone on the "do not call list", but there he was, pretending to be someone else.

It was pathetic and a little scary. I texted him back, "Eric, although I appreciate the effort, this should be the last text we exchange."

I didn't get a text back from him. I suppose looking down at your phone and realizing you just made a complete ass out of yourself is enough to cause at least a little pause. I was lucky, he took the hint. That was the last I saw or heard of the Red Sox Fan.

This showed me that: one, there are creepy people out there, and sometimes they wear clever disguises; and two, that I made an impression. It wasn't one I am one hundred percent proud of, but something made this guy not want to give me up, even though there are millions of playthings in the sea.

16

Gone Fishing

Like so many of my encounters, I met Corey online. What grabbed my attention first was the fact that he produced his own TV programs for Discovery Channel and National Geographic. Corey was a professional fisherman, and he lived about an hour south of where I did.

We started chatting with email at first, which turned into text messaging, which turned into phone calls. We had a ton in common and he made me laugh a lot. He quoted movie lines as much, if not more, than I did.

When I showed his pictures to the girls one night while sipping lattes, I got a lot of positive feedback. Sally and Lucy kept hoping that one of the men I was playing with would end up being Mr. Right.

It was a very encouraging environment in general for me to keep up my fun; I could tell they were secretly hoping for my happy ending. I had a different kind of happy ending in mind for these encounters; with any luck I would have several happy endings with each of them.

> *Whore Tip: Always be yourself, unless of course you're role-playing. Then be whoever your playmate wants you to be, as long as you are comfortable with the role.*

The only person that had something that wasn't completely positive to say was Alex. She looked at the pictures for a minute and then handed the phone back to me. I was waiting for her opinion, but she simply took another long swig from her coffee cup and then tucked a strand of hair behind her ear.

I was confused, she *always* had an opinion. After looking at her with my best confused look, which to my dismay she didn't bother to comment on, I finally asked, "What?" She just simply shrugged. This was irritating and never a good sign.

She took another sip of the coffee.

I did the same, but didn't take my eyes off her.

The other girls had moved on and were talking amongst themselves, and Alex wasn't budging. I had a very hard time not feeling awkward in the silence that had formed between me and Alex. Seriously, who has a test of wills involving lattes?

Unfortunately, both Alex and I are stubborn.

I had to take smaller sips so I didn't run out of coffee. I was not about to let her win this. I am not a good loser.

After a time, the others began to notice our game of sip and stare. Baley looked back and forth between Alex and I, then Sally followed suit. I almost choked on my coffee when I noticed that it looked like they were watching a tennis match.

Finally, Alex cracked. I thought I had won until she stood up, placed her empty cup in the trash bin and said quite confidently, "I am getting a cupcake and your fisherman is gay." She turned and walked towards the counter.

I was more surprised than anything. I wasn't sure how she had come to that conclusion. When I pressed her upon her arrival back to the table with the aforementioned cupcake, she said she could just tell. She said her gaydar worked perfectly.

I should explain at this point that Alex, and well, all of us, have absolutely nothing against any sexual preference. We are an encouraging lot; however, one should not date an opposite-sex same-sex fan, unless they play on both sides of the fence.

Whore Tip: When it comes to a preference or desire for a certain gender in your partner, own it. It is okay to play on either side of the fence as long as you are honest with yourself and your playmate about your intentions.

Alex did not feel that Corey was one of those cases (AKA bisexual), and felt I was setting myself up for disappointment. My argument was, "Why would Corey be interested and pursuing me if he was gay?"

"It is possible he doesn't know," was her quick retort. It was pointless to continue the debate. I knew as well as she did that I was going to meet him. No observations about his sexuality on her part would dissuade me.

The night Corey and I scheduled to meet, I had a small matter to take care of first. My friends and I decided it would be a good idea for all of us to get a matching tattoo, something lasting we could share. We chose the Chinese symbol for friend. Yes, we did verify the symbol meant what it was supposed to, and didn't just pick it out of a book.

Tattoos are permanent. It is very important that you choose something that has significance.

Whore Tip: Never get a name tattooed on your body that is not your child's or your parents. Love, unfortunately, is not always forever and, with a sixty-five percent divorce rate in America, that name has a better chance of expiring than a Twinkie.

There were six of us that met up at the tattoo parlor that fine Saturday night. The tattoo, which we decided to put on our big toe, took less than a minute each.

I wish I could have chosen who went first. The reaction of the first one of us to get tattooed set the stage for the rest. For myself, it was easy and fairly painless. For Sally and Baley, well, they had to be held down. Longest minute of their lives, I believe.

When we finally finished up, I was quick to leave. The girls knew I had a date.

I met Corey at his house. He lived in a condo near the beach, and he'd suggested we could take a little stroll, talk, and see how the chemistry was.

> *Whore Tip: When meeting someone online/phone/ text it is much easier to develop chemistry than it sometimes is in real life. I think because you are part of the creation of who they are, and sometimes the living breathing person is not nearly as amazing as the one you made up.*

Corey looked exactly like his picture. He even had the slight tan lines from wearing sunglasses on the water all the time. He greeted me with a big hug. He was my height and had wavy blond hair. His skin was tan, and he had blue eyes and a sweet smile. He also smelled like the beach. That sounds like a cliché, I know, but he smelled exactly like what I remembered of days spent playing in the waves when I was younger.

He grabbed a couple of cold beers and we headed out for our stroll. It was windy out, but not chilly. Warm breezes can happen quite frequently during the spring and summer months in Florida.

He handed me my beer, and led the way down a small path behind his condo complex to a boat dock and a set of stairs to the beach.

We continued to hit it off in person as much as we had on the phone. We walked in the sand and let the waves come up and cover our feet and ankles. I had worn flip flops due to the tattoo, which was handy.

He was funny and loved musicals almost as much as I did. We even sang a couple of songs from *The Rocky Horror Picture Show*. One of the worst movies ever made, and on my top five list.

I was having an amazing time, but Alex's voice was in my head. I tried to ignore it, and looked for any indication he was not interested in female companionship. I didn't see anything that would lead me to believe he was anything other than what he appeared to be; smart, funny and sexy.

The tattoo hurt like hell. The salt water burned, and I think I whimpered a couple of times when the tide pulled the water across my toe.

When I yelped a little louder than I meant to, Corey asked me what was wrong. I explained the tattoo dilemma and he laughed. I would have done the same thing in his position. He insisted we go back inside and rinse off my foot in his bathtub. I hoped that meant I got to wash everything off in his tub, including our clothes.

When we got back to his apartment he showed me to the tub, turned on the water, made sure it was warm enough for me and then left the bathroom. I assumed he went to get more towels for us to dry off with after our fun.

I got undressed and rinsed off my toe and my legs where there was some sand left over from the beach. After a few minutes of sitting on the tub at a weird angle so I would look sexy and not at all hunched over when he returned, it occurred to me that he wasn't. I wasn't sure what the etiquette was for, "Hello, you left me in the bathroom with a perfect opportunity to get naked. Are you coming back?"

*Whore Tip: Always have a plan, or at least be willing
to improvise without getting too freaked out about it,
even if the plan becomes a mad dash to get the hell out.*

I decided the best thing I could do was turn this to my advantage.
I was already naked and I knew I could make this work. I grabbed
a bath towel and wrapped it around my naked form, turned off the
water and opened the door.

After a bit of searching, I found him sitting on the couch, with
a new beer in hand, watching TV. This was puzzling. When I
approached he turned and said, "Oh, there you are. I was wondering
if you were okay. I was about to come check on you and make sure
you didn't fall in."

He was smiling, and I think he thought he was being funny. I
was officially perplexed, but didn't let it show. That was the first
and, to this point, last time I was in front of a man in a towel and
he didn't insist on seeing what was underneath.

In the sultriest voice I could muster, I replied, "I thought you
might be joining me. I was all wet and waiting." He looked at me
quietly for a few moments. I leaned in, planting my hands on the
edge of the couch, giving a better view of my breasts, barely hidden
under the towel.

He patted the couch next to him, which prompted me to
saunter over and place myself beside him.

Wearing a towel is basically like saying, "Hello, I have no clothes
on, and with one quick pull, I'm all yours." Note that sitting around
in a towel is not as sexy as, say, sitting around in a robe that is loose
and open, exposing flashes of skin in all the right places.

As I sat there next to him, he played with my hair a little bit, and
ran his fingers along my neck.

Then he looked at the TV. It was only for a moment, but
he did look.

I must not have been hiding how perplexed I was, because he asked me, "What are you thinking?"

I wanted to say, "I was wondering why you are not naked and on top of me, or vice versa, right now." Instead, I strategically said, "I was wondering what your lips taste like." Skillfully played, I know.

The night was becoming a true test of my ability to guide a ship to not crash into the iceberg. After you put a certain amount of effort into anything, you feel like you should get your reward.

Whore Tip: The juice should always be worth the squeeze. Otherwise you should never go back for a second glass.

He took the bait, put down his beer, leaned into me, said, "Oh, really?" and kissed me.

His lips were soft and his kiss was almost delicate, which was not a good thing necessarily. A little moan usually helps turn up the passion in any encounter.

The same held true for the man who had his tongue in my mouth. He ran his fingers through my hair and pulled me to him. My hands slid up his chest until my fingers were on his shoulders.

Although we had a rocky start, I could tell that now we had smooth sailing. (I know my boat analogies are terrible, but I also know that I will throw a couple more ashore during this story.)

I was hoping this encounter was going to happen on the couch. I began to lean back and pull him on top of me, but he stood up rather suddenly and briskly pulled me up from the couch.

My towel fell off. Corey paused, and took me in. For the first time I saw hunger in his eyes, and I saw his cock throb against the material of his shorts. I had renewed hope that I wasn't on a deserted island.

He led me into the bedroom where he had a king size bed. The décor was simple, as it had been throughout most of his place.

Bachelors usually have minimal decorations. Sprucing the place up means buying a bigger TV or a new gaming system.

He guided me to the bed. Wrapping his arms around me he kissed me, gently at first, and then let me taste just a little bit of his tongue. He moved my head to the side by gently kissing down my throat to the curve of my shoulder. I was on fire. He was taking his time and exploring every inch of me.

His hands were roaming as well, running his fingertips up my back, and then down again. Grasping my bottom and squeezing, he pulled me into him so I felt his erection pushing against my wetness through his shorts.

Running his hands up my sides, he grasped my breasts, rolling them slowly in his hands, and then tugging at my nipples. Normally, this would drive me crazy.

The way Corey was playing me didn't feel like desire, more like curiosity. It started to get awkward and I let another moan escape my lips. That was what he was looking for, it seemed, as if he was working from a manual, *How to Please a Woman and Stick Your Cock in Her*. The encounter was continuing to be weird.

He stopped his nipple explorations, pulled off his shirt and cast it aside. He spun me around and guided me onto the bed so that I was on my knees. With the sound of a zipper, I heard the fabric of his shorts hit the floor. I made sure my feet were positioned off the bed and not touching anything. My toe was still sore from the tattoo, sand and salt water; it didn't need more pain inflicted upon it that night.

With as much speed as he could, he slid a condom onto his mainmast and I felt the tip of his cock touch my wet folds. "Oh, god yes!" tumbled out of my mouth as a wave of need washed over me and I threw my head back.

He glided into me, gently and slowly, as if he thought I would break, or he wasn't used to doing this. It was too slow for me, and I was thinking again, so I pushed back against him, showing him

I wanted and could take more. He began to push harder, in and out, thrusting deeper. I rocked against him, finding the motion of the ocean and moving with it. He found his rhythm and I brought my fingers to my clit. Balancing on just my knees and one arm, I touched myself. I felt the familiar tingle as my touch sent pulses from my clit through my entire being.

> *Whore Tip: Know how to please yourself. If you are afraid or unable to make yourself cum, then you will never know what feels best and how to guide your partner there.*

Thrusting harder and faster against him, making him keep up with my need, my moans got louder. His hands grasped my hips firmly, as if afraid that letting go, even slightly, would cause him to fall off of me. I came, hard. I dug my fingers into his bed as my legs began to shake. I felt him explode inside me, and then, without a word or gesture, he was out of me and heading to the bathroom, closing the door behind him.

I collapsed on the bed, letting myself feel the sensations still coursing through me. It didn't take long for my mind to interrupt me with the fact that, after several minutes, Corey hadn't returned to the room.

I sat up and looked down on the floor to see his clothes weren't there, either. Had he taken them with him? This was turning out to not be the evening I had expected.

I got up and gently knocked on the bathroom door; no response. I opened the door carefully, not wanting to walk in on him taking a dump. Nothing. The other door that led out of the bathroom was open. My clothes were neatly stacked on the counter of the bathroom.

Getting cleaned up and dressed, I started to get annoyed and a little mad about what had just happened. Before I opened the door to head out, I got myself into the correct frame of mind.

I looked at myself in the mirror. This encounter was nothing more than that, an encounter, I told myself. I couldn't always predict how they would go down, and each was going to be different. I knew this. I also knew that if I did anything other than walk out the bathroom door, grab my bag and leave, I would want to unravel this puzzle. The unraveling, however, would be a violation of the point of having these types of friends.

I honestly didn't care what the weirdness was. Did it matter if it was him or if it was me? No, it didn't. Even if it was something I had done, that wouldn't matter to the next guy. Each one would perceive me though their eyes and what they desired. I wasn't giving this any more time.

With that resolution, I opened the door to the bathroom and walked into the living room. He was again seated on the couch, beer in hand. When I approached, he turned and said, "Oh, there you are. I was wondering if you were okay. I was about to come check on you." Déjà Idiot.

I leaned in, kissed him on the cheek, grabbed my bag and headed to the door. Before he said anything, I turned and said, "Thanks" and walked out.

One of the nuggets of wisdom taken from any situation like this is that you are in control. You can decide to be affected by what is going on, or you can decide you got what you came for (or didn't), but you don't have to watch the movie all the way to the end. You can dock that boat and walk ashore.

17

CAPSIZED

I spent the time driving home thinking about how weird the night had been. There was a little nagging thought that kept creeping into my mind. I had never heard of a night quite like that before. I could see Alex sitting across from me, sipping her latte and telling me the one thing my brain didn't want to hear.

The next day I met up with Alex and Sally to get pedicures. After getting a tattoo the previous night, and then drenching it in the ocean, it was not a good idea.

Sally always takes what seemed like years to pick out her nail color. The wait was building until I finally blurted out, "He is gay."

Sally looked confused, a break from wincing in pain from the soothing minerals. "Who's gay?" she asked.

"The Fisherman," Alex said as she looked over at me and smirked. I couldn't tell what bothered me more, that she was right and knew it, or that I could have seen it too if I had been willing to look.

Sally asked for the details, so I told them both about the night. Agreeing that it was awkward, and loving my live quotes, they both helped me to laugh about it. Talking to them removed any self-doubt that may have lingered.

Corey called me later that week and wanted to know if I would like to go out for a boat ride. I had, of course, flagged him in my phone to make sure I was never tempted to make that mistake again.

I didn't return, the call and that was the last time I heard from him. Flipping through the channels on TV one night, I saw him on the local news. He was describing an incident with a shark while fishing. I couldn't help think that I hoped he was able to finally reel in the big one, his Moby Dick!

18

Possibly Some
Bad Choices

I met Mark online. The details of meeting Mark were not what fascinated me. It was more how interesting it was getting to know him.

He was thirty-seven years old, six-foot-two, and had brown hair and eyes. In his picture he had a goatee and mustache. I like to call it the pirate look. I would not say he was cute or gorgeous, but he was handsome. This descriptive is usually saved for different kinds of men. You would never say that Vin Diesel is cute, but he is gorgeous.

Mark worked in sales for a beverage distributor. He did regional sales, and seemed like a professional business man. I had not met a lot of those in my life.

We began speaking via email. Mark was witty and entertaining. He wasn't looking for anything serious and since neither was I; it was the beginning of another Mr. OK for Now.

This is what I had taken to calling the men in my life.

After asking him if he was married or gay, both questions he answered with a resounding "no", I suggested we chat via text, always easier. He suggested we use an instant messaging service. I wasn't opposed, as it had a feature you could turn on that allowed messages to come as texts.

He told me that he was recently divorced, and that his now ex-wife had been adventurous at first, but then turned out to be very frigid after the marriage. He wanted someone who was up for sexual adventures. I asked him to explain in more detail. I had experienced Red Sox, and that was a whole level of adventure I wasn't ready to take on again.

Mark told me he had fantasies around dominating his partner. He wasn't into S&M or pain, he simply wanted to have the girl wanting him so badly she was begging for it, and he wanted the control always, unless he chose to give it. I told him the only way that could work was if he was able to bring his partner to the point of ecstasy regularly and easily. He assured me of his prowess.

In the relationships I was creating, if you wanted to categorize them as that, being yourself and stating exactly what you want is not only encouraged, it is required.

> *Whore Tip: You will more likely get exactly what you want or something better if you are willing to ask for it. If you don't ask you will never know the possibilities.*

Talking with Mark, I told him exactly what I liked and how I liked it. He told me he would give me anything I wanted, as long as I begged for it like a "good girl". I could play that part.

The flip side to being exactly who you are in the bedroom is to ensure your partner is encouraged to be exactly who they are as well. Allowing them to be free to say and do those things that make them happy or horny is how you get the best out of them. If they feel they have to be careful around you, then you won't get everything they can be.

I decided I wanted to talk to Mark. I only had the one picture of him from his profile and while he was fun to play with via text and email, sending naughty messages throughout the day, I wanted to see how far this would go.

He agreed to call me one afternoon. When the phone rang around the time we discussed it was from a blocked number, not a good sign. I answered assuming it was him. Normally, I never take calls from a blocked number; you shouldn't either. Even if someone calls from jail to bail them out, the number isn't blocked.

"Hello," I answered. If I had been sure it was him, I would have readied a far more sensual greeting, but one has to be sure before using amazing flirtation methods. It could have been someone trying to get me to buy a vacation home.

"Hi, is this Randi?" a deep male voice asked.

"Yes. Is this Mark?" I replied, adding a little more sex into my voice.

Whore Tip: Using your voice to turn your partner on can be all it takes. It is the same as using the right look to make them all warm and tingly. Never underestimate the little things.

"Wow, you sound even sexier than I imagined," he said. That is always a wonderful compliment. I thanked him.

I should probably mention that I was actually driving to Orlando. This, for those who do not know the greater Florida metropolitan areas, is about a two-hour drive without traffic and going the speed limit, which I never do.

"So, what are you doing?" Mark asked me. I really wish I could have told him something like playing in a bubble bath, but I had the less sexy answer of, "driving to a convention for work." He laughed a little.

Mark's laugh was deep and throaty. I could tell instantly that he would be able to use simple whispers in that voice and it would turn up the ecstasy in any sexual situation.

We bantered a bit back and forth, flirting. I could tell he was asking me things to see if I was what I appeared to be in our email interactions. As with any online interaction, whether via text or email, when you finally get to interact with the person live, you see if they can live up to the idea you created of them in your head.

If anyone tells you that they don't have expectations, they are either a liar or the most boring person on the planet.

Something you have to be careful of is not to design the person in your mind beyond what they can live up to. This is one of the easiest traps a person who is "playing" can do. They don't see and get to know their partner for *who they are*, and not the embodiment of what they *wished they were*. That's when you end up disappointed that they didn't live up to the fantasy version you had of them. You can also easily ignore red flags when you do this, flags that tell you to walk away. Don't paint a picture over the original art work. You won't see what is really there.

> *Whore Tip: Let the person be who they are and see if that can surprise you. Having no expectations is not the same as having low expectations. Make sure you know the difference.*

After my answers assuaged his fears, he dropped a bit of a bombshell on me. "Randi, I need to tell you something before this goes any further," he said, his tone changing to something less sensual.

My armor started to go up. After the married man incident, as I referred to it, I wasn't interested in being thrown in that situation again. I had already asked Mark if he was married and he had told me no, but that didn't always guarantee the truth.

"Okay," I replied. The 'okay' was drawn out and I knew my tone sounded defensive. I didn't care. If he was playing with me, in the not-good way, then my tone was the least of his problems.

"I don't know how to say this exactly..." he paused. I said nothing. "The picture on my profile, that... well... that isn't me." I expected him to continue, but he didn't. I was more thrown off by this admission than I would have been if he had told me he was married. I had been prepared for the married comment. I was not prepared for this. The phone was silent for almost a minute.

Whore Tip: Always, always, trust your gut.

"Randi? Are you still there?" he asked. I heard the worry in his voice.

"Yep," I replied. I heard Alex's voice in my head, "*Who cares if that was not his picture, find out if he some kind of troglodyte. If not, see if he is doable.*" She always has such a way with words.

"So...what do you look like? Are you a hideous troll and that is why you used a fake picture?" As I asked, I tried to put some playfulness in my voice.

I heard a sigh as he let out the breath he must have been holding. I sensed that we had gone farther than he thought we would, and he hadn't thought this conversation would happen.

"You're not mad?" he asked.

"I haven't decided if I am mad," I replied. "I am incredibly turned on by you so far, and if that changes, and you turn me off physically or vice versa, that will be disappointing. I don't think I will end up being mad, though." As the words left my lips I realized they were true. I wouldn't end up mad.

He didn't owe me anything and I didn't owe him either. That was part of the fun of these types of relationships.

Whore Tip: Finding playmates requires skill, willing-ness and an ability not to get attached. The emotions should be the kind stimulating your mind and your loins, never your heart.

"So, that begs the question... what do you look like?" I asked, putting a little dominance in my tone. I knew this would bring back the naughty side of him. He laughed a little at that, then began the description.

He described himself as six-foot-four with sandy blond hair that he kept short and blue eyes. That all sounded good so far.

He then, hesitantly, said that he was overweight, more than just a few extra pounds. I asked him to give me a weight. I knew that wasn't always the best gauge, but it would give me an idea.

After a pause he said close to three-hundred-pounds. He was a big boy, but he was also tall, so the height-to-weight ratio wasn't horrible. I wasn't deterred yet. "Ok, so what else?" I said.

"I was born with a harelip. I had surgery when I was younger but I have a scar." I could tell by his tone that his defenses were down. He had exposed himself on a level that was touchier then sex, which isn't the norm. Even if that had been a deal breaker for me, which it wasn't, I couldn't be mean to him now.

"Ok, so is that it?" I asked. My tone wasn't enough to let him know that we were okay to play yet.

"Yes, yes that is all," he said quietly.

"Mark," I said.

"Yeah?" he replied.

"Thank you for telling me. That would have surprised me when we met, and I would rather spend the first few minutes taking my clothes off for you, instead of trying to figure out why you weren't honest with me to begin with." He laughed. All was good.

"So do I get a picture now?" I asked. "Of the real you?"

Instead of saying yes, he told me he had a fantasy, one that he had been thinking about for years. My ears perked up.

Here was his fantasy:

It starts with meeting in a hotel room. The woman, me in this case, was already there. As he was driving to the hotel, he wanted to talk. The conversation was to start with a me briefly describing the layout of the room, and then rapidly move on to his describing in detail what he wanted to do to me; I was to listen and be touching myself while wearing lace panties.

The second part to his fantasy involved my masturbation bringing me to climax, at least once, so that the panties became very wet.

When he arrived at the hotel, he wanted me to take the panties off and place them on the door handle, leaving the door so it was slightly ajar. All of the lights were to be off and the curtains closed. I should be lying on the bed naked, waiting for him.

He would remove the panties from the door, and close it. The room would then be pitch black. He would find his way to the bed and by touch, he would move up my body, starting with my feet, then my calves, up my thighs seeking out my wet mound and tasting me. He would give me pleasure orally until I came, all over his face and fingers, and then the lights were to be turned on. He finished by saying he knew I would have to be beyond trusting of him, a total stranger, and that he understood if I wasn't willing.

Just hearing that, I was wet. I could see why that would be a fantasy of his. I could also see where he was correct; I would have to suspend any caution I had to fulfill this fantasy.

I told him I would like to think about it.

He let me know that my decision would not change the fact that he still wanted to meet me, but if I was willing, that fantasy is what he would choose.

I told him to give me a couple of days and I would let him know what my decision was.

The moment I hung up I called Alex. After I explained the situation, she told me she wanted to think about it as well. She saw the allure, but there were more unknowns than usual. Alex asked me if I had told anyone else and I told her she was my first call. After a couple more questions she recommended getting everyone together for coffee. While ultimately my decision, she thought getting various points of view might help to make the decision clearer (or more convoluted), but it was worth a shot.

> *Whore Tip: Any choice you make in a relationship of any kind, make sure it's the choice that you want to make. You can always get advice from friends, or even strangers, but when it comes down to it, you do what YOU want and not what another tells you to.*

I sent a mass text to the girls: "Coffee tomorrow tonight. Seven o'clock, usual place. Need to convene the council of the elders." This might have been melodramatic, but Sally found it incredibly funny. Alex, Sally, Lucy and Baley all said they would be there. I love my friends.

The next night, after we grabbed our coffee and treats, I guided us to a less public table near the back of the café area. I don't actually care what people think of me or my exploits, but there were some students studying, and ladies meeting for their crochet club. I didn't want to get us banned from our favorite hangout.

"So, ladies, you are most likely wondering why I have called you here," I said, after finishing a bite of the oatmeal cookie I had chosen to go with my latte this evening.

Sally and Lucy laughed, Alex sighed and I think Baley almost spit out the sip she had just taken. "I have been given an opportunity. Under the advice of Alex, I want to get your opinion of what you think I should do."

With that, I laid out all of the details for them. When I finished, I was surprised that no one had any questions, with the exception of Sally, who asked, "What do you want to do?" I told her that I thought I wanted to do it, but I also knew that my current mindset was not always conducive to the best choices. It would be good for the girls to tell me what they thought.

After a little weighing of the pros and cons, they agreed that if it was something I felt comfortable doing, then I should do it. None of the girls felt like it was something they could do, but as Baley stated, it wasn't because she didn't want to be able to, she just wasn't as willing to pursue adventures the way I was. I smiled when she said that. I took it as a compliment.

The next day I texted Mark, "So which hotel were you thinking?"

He immediately texted me back, "YES!"

It is always cute how excited boys get about new toys, I thought, and laughed.

19

PANTIES ON THE DOOR

ark called me later that night to find out if I had a preference where the hotel was located. I preferred one off of a
major street because it would be easier to get to. He chose
a five-star hotel right off of the highway. We decided to meet Friday
night. Sally had a book reading that night, which I had agreed to
go to. I let Mark know I would need to be gone for about an hour at
nine pm, unless he wanted to put off our encounter? He was much
more willing to miss me for the hour than wait any longer.

I gave all the details to Sally, including the timing, which was
standard. I even texted the hotel room number when I arrived.
Because there was so much more risk involved it was important to
have someone know where I was.

*Whore Tip: Safety, whether with condoms or location,
is always first.*

There was a part of me that couldn't believe I was actually going
through with this. A larger part of me couldn't wait for it to happen.
He paid for the room online and in my name, and even called in
advance to make sure that all I needed to do was pick up my key.

I arrived at the hotel around six pm and as agreed, I texted him
as I was checking in. When I was getting ready for the night, I made

sure my make-up was perfectly slutty. My eyes were lined with black liquid liner, and I used smoky grey colors with a hint of purple to accent my hazel eyes. I also put on my favorite red lipstick.

Whore Tip: Stay-on make-up, especially lip color, should always be in your arsenal. It is important that at any stage of playing, you look fabulous and your partner doesn't end up wearing your shade!

My outfit was much simpler. I wore jeans, a tank top, flip-flops and a hoodie. My outer clothes weren't important. When he saw, or felt, me for the first time, I wouldn't be wearing anything. I did acquire the perfect bra and panty set for this tryst, red with black lace accents, to match my lip color.

The room was laid out like most hotel rooms, the bathroom was on the left as I walked in, and in the main room the bed was against the right wall with a dresser and TV opposite. There was a desk just past the bend, and a smaller table with two chairs in front of the window. I texted him the layout of the room. One of the easiest ways to kill the mood of the evening was if he had to fumble around, running into things trying to get to me.

The bed was king size, which would be the most comfortable considering both of our sizes. I took some time as I undressed to figure out the best position for me to be in when he arrived.

Almost on cue, when I was dressed only in a bra and panties, my phone rang.

Butterflies leapt in my belly. I took a deep breath and answered. Before I could even speak he asked, "Are you on the bed waiting for me?"

"Yes."

"Good girl," he said.

I could hear the hunger in his voice. I knew that *I* was what was going to make this either good or mind-blowing. I wanted the latter, and with that the butterflies were gone. The next words simply flowed from my lips. "Tell me what to do," I asked in a husky voice.

"How much do you want me, baby?" he asked.

I was already wet for him. He told me how his cock had become hard several times that day thinking about what was going to happen, and as bad as he had wanted the release he saved it, all for me.

He started giving me instructions, and I did exactly as I was told. I let my fingers slide between my legs and touch my lips, already very wet with desire. I felt for my spot, sending tingles through my entire body. Moans began escaping my lips. He listened as I brought myself to climax. I ran my fingers on top of the panties, pushing against my wetness.

The second time I finished he told me he was in the lobby and that it was time to get myself completely ready for him, and hung up the phone.

I got out of the bed and removed the bra I had been wearing and placed it on the pile of clothes stacked on one of the chairs near the window. Before I opened the door, I slid my panties off. Standing behind the door I flipped the slide lock, preventing the door, from closing all the way. I put my wet panties on the handle and went back to the bed to get into position. I switched the lamp off and waited.

It wasn't long before the sliver of light coming from the door was blocked. He was there. My heart was pounding in my chest. Even though I was confident, I was nervous. That small voice reminded me that this could go horribly wrong. I told it to shut up.

He opened the door and, because of where the bed was located, he wasn't able to see me, nor I him. He then closed the door, leaving the room pitch black.

"Your panties are so very wet and you smell amazing," he said. His voice even more husky in person. I got goose bumps all over. I wasn't supposed to speak, except when he wanted me to. He had asked for complete control, and so far I was more than willing to give it to him. I heard him moving around as he made his way into the room.

It is interesting having only certain senses available. As I lay there, I wondered if he was going to undress before touching me, or if he was going to make me wait. Since we couldn't see each other it would be about the pleasure, the thrill. In most scenarios you get to see if the person is physically attractive to you. For us, we were going to see if our imaginations and physical reactions could fuel the heat.

Whore Tip: It is never about looks alone. You will find that will only take you so far. If the personality or skill set is terrible, it won't matter if they are perfect on the eyes.

As these thoughts were tumbling through my head, I was startled when he grabbed the sheets and threw them off me. His fingertips started playing up my legs until they almost touched my waiting wetness. A small moan escaped my lips and I reached my hands under the pillow my head was resting on. I knew myself well enough to know I would reach out if not constrained.

"How bad do you want me baby?" he asked as he moved up running his hands along my stomach up to my breasts, taking my nipples between his fingers and gently tugging.

Another moan. "So bad... please," was my reply.

He laughed, knowing he was getting exactly what he wanted. I was his to play with.

He withdrew his hands and I could hear him moving down the bed again. He pushed my legs apart, and I felt his weight on the end of the bed. He lifted one of my feet to his lips, and gently kissed the top of my foot to my ankle. His tongue occasionally licking, he did this all the way to the back of my knees. He seemed to know every sensitive spot. He repeated his kisses on my other leg, and then pushed my legs up, bending them at the knee.

I held on to the sides of the pillow as each touch pushed me closer to climax. He was deliberate in each action; knowing how to bring me closer while keeping me just far enough away to tease. I felt myself throbbing between my legs. Then his lips were on my thigh, gently kissing and licking at first, and then I felt his teeth as he got closer.

A small scream escaped my lips when he bit me a little harder. "I won't ask you if you want me to stop... I have no intention of stopping. You are mine," he said as he bit me again. It was hard but not painful, and my back arched: I was so close.

Then his mouth was hovering just above my wet folds, so close I could feel his breath. "Tell me how much you need me right now," he said, hovering, his warm breath sending shivers through me.

"Oh God... More!" was all I could say.

I wanted to reach out and take control. I wanted his lips to taste mine, I wanted him to push himself inside of me, and I wanted to touch myself as he watched. I wanted to explode.

His lips finally touched the exact spot I needed them to. He slid his hands under my ass and pushed me harder against his mouth. In moments I climaxed. My back arched, my legs were trembling and I dug my fingertips into the sheets on each side of me. Uncontrollable sounds escaped my lips as he held onto me, and rode through my waves of pleasure.

"Wow," I said. My voice was strained as I realized how dry my throat was.

There is something indescribable about having an encounter such as the one we shared. There is empowerment in the willingness to give yourself over to the danger of trusting someone you have never met before.

You might be thinking that I am completely insane. A part of me just might be. What I chose to do with Mark could have had many negative outcomes, but luckily that is not what happened. I would never give advice other than to trust yourself and your judgment. I did. I listened to my inner voice and did exactly what I wanted to do. Of course, my inner voice was purring.

Whore Tip: You know yourself and what you are comfortable with more than anyone else. If you're asked to do or be something that is not to your liking, you always have the power. Simply say no.

"Do you need some water?" he asked, gently rubbing his hand on my leg. That sent shivers throughout my whole body; I was still very sensitive to the touch. "Yes, please," I replied.

"Light," he said. The moment of truth, I thought to myself. I mentally crossed my fingers and hoped that when I saw his face I wouldn't regret one of the best orgasms of my life.

I switched the light on and closed my eyes, not exactly out of fear, although there was a little, but I knew I would be blind at first. I slowly opened my eyes to see him for the first time.

He matched his description. I would love to say I opened my eyes and was blown away by how amazing he looked, or that he was one of those people who describe themselves as average but are really gorgeous.

That was not the case with Mark. He was tall, he had sandy-blond hair, he was slightly overweight, and he had a scar on his upper lip from the surgery he had told me about.

I could tell from the look on his face that he was vulnerable, and waiting to see my reaction. I did exactly what I needed to do in order to make sure he knew just how much I appreciated the pleasure he had just given me. I smiled and winked. "Nice to meet you, Mark."

I could tell this pleased him and alleviated any worry he might have had. I thought about how many times a person doesn't think about what the *other* person may be feeling in regards to their confidence or comfort. It can be very easy to get wrapped up one's own insecurities.

He licked his lips a little and said, "You taste as good as you look." This sent a new wave of shivers through me. He continued, "I want to clean you off. Go into the shower and wait for me."

As I walked into the bathroom, I deliberately closed the door only partway. I turned on the shower and made sure it was hot, but not scalding. Steam began to billow from the shower, and I stepped in and pulled the shower curtain across the rod as loudly as possible. I wasn't sure how long he would make me wait, but I knew I had to leave clues or this little game would never work.

He didn't make me wait long. When I heard him enter the bathroom, I turned to face the shower head, already sufficiently wet for more than one reason.

As he stepped into the shower behind me, he ran his hands from my shoulders down to my waist. Once his hands were just above my hips, he pulled me back into him. "I am going to clean you and then I am going to make you dirty again," he whispered into my ear. With his size, even I felt small and very feminine next to him.

I am very much the female vixen, but when you are as tall or taller than most of the men around you, you rarely get to feel like the "delicate flower". When it does happen, it is nice.

I turned and looked up into his eyes and nodded. He smiled and began to clean me slowly and sensually. He took his time, enjoying every inch of me, now and then kissing or nibbling some area he found appetizing.

When he had finished, including my hair, he kissed my lips. Gently at first and then pushing his tongue in deeply, drinking me in, holding me against him as water flowed down my shoulders and back.

He pulled away from me and pulled back the shower curtain. "I want you to dry off and be ready for me," he said, and nodded towards the door. I climbed out of the tub, grabbed a towel and headed back into the room. I checked myself in the mirror inside the closet to ensure I didn't look like a raccoon.

*Whore Tip: If you get to play in the water, remember
your hair and make-up are the first casualties. Take
a moment to straighten your look out as much as possible so you don't look like a mug shot.*

Luckily, I had to only wipe away a little smeared mascara
and I was set. My lips were still red and my skin had a nice glow
from the hot water. I climbed back into the bed just as I heard the
shower shut off.

When he emerged, he was dried and naked. That was the first
time I got to see all of him. If I was dating, Mark wouldn't be my
type. That may seem shallow, but in my defense, and the defense of
anyone that chooses to have experiences similar to mine, the person
you have chosen doesn't have to be Mr. (or Ms.) Right. You are
looking for a Mr. Okay for Now.

Taking all of him in as he stood there, Mark began to stroke
himself as he told me to come to him. I did, but, as I got up, I
sneaked a look at the time. It was seven-twenty pm. The fantasy
could continue for another hour or so, but then I had to leave for
the book reading.

*Whore Tip: Real friends and family are always more
important than sex. Never put your orgasmic bliss in
front of a promise you have made.*

I moved over and put myself in front of him. He continued to
stroke himself while he began to touch me. Eventually reaching his
fingers between my legs and the wet folds awaiting him, he stroked
himself a little faster as he pushed his fingers inside of me. I moaned
again. He leaned in, licking my neck up to my ear. "You will pleasure me," he whispered, as a guttural sound escaped him. He moved
and grabbed a condom I hadn't noticed from under the pillow on

the bed. He slid it on and then lay back on the bed, beckoning me to mount him.

I climbed up and straddled his hips, tilting my body to lean in. Kissing down his chest, I was able to angle to grab hold of him and slide him inside of me. The moan came from him this time. I sat back up, sliding him deep inside of me. My back arched as I began to move up and down on his shaft. With each stroke, I would rub up against him, creating the friction I needed to bring on a series of orgasmic explosions.

> *Whore Tip: Not all playmates are as good at the game as you are, so make sure you can compensate for lousy skills with your own exceptional technique. If you know those positions that bring you pleasure you, can almost always bring about a happy ending.*

As I rode Mark like the good girl he wanted, he grabbed my thighs to hold on. Inside of me, I could feel him thicken as he got closer to his own explosion. So I did the one thing I could for both of us–I went faster and pushed harder. I exploded in an orgasm, and my hands went to his chest to steady my motions as he came, grinding my hips to get him as deep inside of me as possible.

I rode my orgasm until I began to quiet and then rolled off of him and landed on the bed. I needed to regain my breath and steady the blood flow through my limbs. I slowly got up on trembling legs and grabbed a water bottle off of the table. I heard Mark move behind me, I assumed to remove the condom and clean up from the recent events.

As I made my way back over to the bed to sit, he came and sat beside me. He placed a hand on my leg, leaned in and kissed me lightly on the lips. "Thank you, Randi," he said, adding another kiss.

"You are most welcome," I replied and smiled at him.

He continued, "I know I asked a lot of you to do this. I just want you to know that I appreciate this whole night, and you for being willing to put yourself out there and trust the whole situation."

I nodded. "Well, it has been quite worth it." With that my playful grin came out. Although I could appreciate his gratitude, I also didn't want to ruin the passion of the moment with anything that remotely related to a feeling. The only feelings I wanted to have involved orgasms. I checked the clock and saw that it was almost time to get ready.

The most dangerous part of defining a line between playmate and relationship is the feelings part. It doesn't mean that you shouldn't have any, we all do. You can like the person, but if you get attached... you are done for.

20

The Book Reading

"So, hoping this doesn't sound as selfish as I think it will, I have to go out to that thing I told you about. I won't be long, but I have to do this," I said. That had been the plan all along, but it sounded terrible when I said it out loud.

"I'll drive you. It is at a coffee shop right?" He was not being dominant. I could tell from how his voice changed, more like the real Mark, not the bedroom Mark.

This threw me off a little, actually it threw me off a lot, and I sat there quiet for a minute. In none of the plans I had played out in my head was him coming with me an option. Sally would be at the reading, and bringing Mark would "cross the streams", as they say. I wasn't sure I was ready for my playmates to meet my real-life friends.

"Randi?" Mark said with a little concern now in his voice.

"Yeah... I mean yes. Are you sure you want to meet my friends?" I asked.

"Why not?" he asked, as if it was simple. "Meeting a friend, they don't know who I am." And there it was. Mark thought that I had kept this as our little secret between us. He didn't know that Sally knew who he was and what was to transpire that night.

I felt my face begin to flush slightly as I blurted out, "You're right, let's do this." I stood, walked to the bathroom and closed the door.

Sitting on the toilet trying to pee, I felt a weird sensation that could have been labeled nervousness, but I knew it was more than that.

On the toilet, with my panties around my calves it hit me. I had never thought of how talking about my little encounters to my friends would affect the playmates if they found out. BI had been different; I had told him about my friends and how we discussed what he and I were up to. But he was young and took it as a compliment. How would Mark take it if he found out? I didn't know what my next move should be. I could keep my mouth closed about not keeping it closed, or fess up and hope it didn't get any more awkward for me then it already had. So I did the best thing I could, absolutely nothing. I peed, pulled my big girl panties back on, washed my hands and got ready for a coffee and a book reading.

As we drove to the coffee shop I almost texted Sally, but I wasn't sure how keen Mark's eyesight was or how to phrase what was about to happen in one quick sentence. How do you tell a friend you are bringing a playmate that she knows all about, but he doesn't know that *she* knows anything, and tell your friend not ask him too many questions because you don't want him to know too much about your real life? It was too complicated for anything but an exasperated sigh, which came out of my mouth as we pulled into the parking lot. Mark asked me if I was okay. I played it off that I was just parched from all of our activity and that I needed something to drink.

> *Whore Tip: Thinking on your feet and ensuring that you give no cause to have your partner think you are anything but amazing and confident is a key Whore talent.*

The coffee shop was located in a strip mall near the college campus. It was a local favorite hangout for the students as it was open every night till one am and had free Wi-Fi. These are two key elements in finishing any midterm. It also boasts one of the best open mic nights for local authors.

As we walked in, there was a coffee bar along one wall with barstools. Everywhere else had couches, chairs and coffee tables that looked like they were all acquired from a secondhand store. The only exception was a six-foot square near the entrance that was the stage.

We made our way further in and heard a guy with shaggy brown hair read a poem from a very worn looking notebook. The poem was about a lost love, which seems like what most poems are about. As we approached the bar to place our order, there was a round of applause when the reader finished.

There were two servers behind the bar, one male and one female. Both had their hair in dreadlocks, tattoos and were dressed like hippies. It occurred to me that it could be the required uniform, but the dreads seemed like a lot of work for a uniform.

I looked at the menu and picked a coffee called the "Mud Puddle Mash-up." It was a latte with two shots of espresso, chocolate and caramel syrup, with a shot of Kahlua then foamed with chocolate milk and topped with a sprinkling of almond powder. The drink seemed ridiculous, but the evening seemed to be going where it wanted, so I might as well keep taking it to the extreme. Mark ordered a black coffee. I guessed he wasn't as adventurous with his drinks as he was with his penis.

While he was paying, I turned to scan the room. As I did, Sally came up and gave me a hug. "I'm so glad you're here," she whispered. "I am a little nervous."

I hugged her back and said, "You will be amazing, and of course I am here, that's what friends do."

Mark turned around as the hug ended and handed me a glass of water. "Your Mud-Puddle drink is going to take a couple of minutes, and I know you're thirsty."

I took the glass with a, "Thank you." I took a sip to keep up the pretense of immense thirst and enjoyed the look on Sally's face as she realized what was standing before her. It was the moment of truth.

"Sally, this is my friend Mark," I said, gesturing towards Mark with my free hand, a playful grin on my face. "Mark, this is Sally, the author friend of mine we are here to see."

"Nice to meet you, Mark," Sally said reaching out her hand for him to shake.

Mark shook her hand. "Nice to meet you. I am looking forward to hearing your work." He played the part of a new friend perfectly.

Sally was up next, so I grabbed my coffee treat and Mark, and I found seats on the couch as close as we could to the stage. I drank what was one of the most amazing coffee confections of my life.

Mark leaned in and whispered, "I can't imagine that your sweet drink tastes as good as you do. I can't wait to have my face between your legs again soon." Shivers went down my spine. This man could turn me on with just words. It didn't hurt that I knew how good he was at tasting me.

Mark kept whispering little notions of what he wanted to do to me when we returned to the room. It made it very hard to concentrate on the reading, but I did my best. When Sally finished, I made sure her applause was the loudest so far. She walked off the stage and came up to us as we stood up from the couch.

"Thank you guys, again, for coming," she said.

"I wouldn't have missed it," I said giving her another hug. Sally said she needed to get home and was going to head out. I knew she didn't have to do any such thing and was letting me head back to my playdate with minimal awkwardness.

21

No Sleep

We headed back to the hotel, and I didn't get three steps in the door before Mark pushed me against the wall and was pulling my pants off. When he had me stripped from the waist down, he unzipped his pants, pulled out his very erect cock, slid on a condom and pushed me against the wall. He lifted one of my legs for a better angle as his mouth found mine. I felt the intoxicating hunger, which for me is one of my biggest turn-ons. He thrust inside of me hard and fast, using the wall to support me as he pushed deeper inside of me with every thrust until I felt him erupt.

After a few more rounds, we both decided it was time to get a little sleep. As I lay next to him, I was glad to find he wasn't a cuddler. It is always awkward to try to avoid a cuddle.

Whore Tip: Cuddling is very intimate. When you are cuddling it is for comfort and safety, which exposes more emotions than giving oral. So cuddle wisely.

As I curled up in the bed thinking I that I would get some of the best sleep I had in a while, being as satisfied as I was, I made an unhappy discovery. Mark snored. Not a little snore either, it was like a buzz saw. At first I tried to cover my head with a pillow, but that wasn't enough. I tried nudging him a little to get him to roll over, anything to get the racket to end. It didn't work.

The unfortunate end to the night was no sleep for me. I spent the entire night unable to block out any of the noise. It was almost as if he got louder no matter what I did. I wanted to leave, but that guilty part of me couldn't do it.

In the morning, when he woke up, I was already dressed. I made up a little white lie about a friend in need and having to head out.

That was not the plan. He wanted to play a little more and tried every way he could to get me to stay. I, however, had been done at four-thirty am after three hours of snoring. He should have been happy I waited until 8:00 am when I dropped my water bottle on the table by "accident" as I was packing.

Whore Tip: Never take for granted that food and sleep = a happy body. If you're going to have adventures, always make sure you keep your body happy, because if it is not happy, you will not be on your best behavior.

I kissed him goodbye and told him to call me later.

22

IF AT FIRST YOU DON'T SLEEP...

After some much needed sleep, I called Sally and we had a good laugh about the night before. She mentioned that he hadn't seemed like my type, and I told her he was very good in the areas I needed him to be, with the exception of sleeping. She laughed and told me I shouldn't plan sleepovers with him again. I agreed.

Later that night Mark texted me and wanted to know how much I missed his cock. It was the dominant part reasserting itself. I knew that the way I had left him had taken a little wind out of his sails.

Since I was finally rested, I was able to handle this with some proper Whoreness. I texted him back: "I have been missing your cock since you last slid it inside of me. My pussy is aching for it."

He responded with: "Of course you are." He wanted to know when I could see him again, and I told him the next weekend.

It was a little annoying that he had to call me. Even after our night of naughtiness, I didn't have his phone number. He said it was all part of his wanting to be in control. In case you were wondering, my red flags were going off a little.

Whore Tip: Red flags are just that. If they start to fly, walk away. That little voice that starts them flying knows something.

I met him at another hotel the next weekend. This time we met earlier in the day to play. He wanted me to stay the night, but I was hesitant to put myself through that again. It seemed to me that it was better to end the night on an exhausted orgasmic high than put myself through the torture of lack of sleep and an agitated morning of driving home. Mark however, was adamant. He had paid for the hotel and wanted to enjoy me in the morning, and since I had skipped out on morning sex the last time, he wanted to cash in that voucher.

Begrudgingly, I stayed. The night was fun, and Mark was just as good a playmate as the first time. Unfortunately, with the distraction of the coffee shop absent, and more time on our hands because of arriving earlier in the day, we ended up with time to talk. When speaking about lovers, idle tongues are reality's playground. I ended up knowing more than I wanted to about Mark.

At first he talked about his job. He seemed more interested in talking about himself than hearing about me, with the exception of my sexual fantasies. Those he wanted to hear all about.

I never come out and flatly admit that I am sleeping with more than one person at a time, but I also never deny it. It is very tacky to pretend that the man you're with is the only one. Deceit is never sexy, no matter what someone thinks the rules of the game are. When Mark asked me if I was seeing anyone else, I told him that I had other playmates.

At first, he seemed a little put off. We were lying on the bed, my head on his chest after our latest round. When I answered, he got very quiet. I wasn't sure what to do or say. I didn't feel bad or guilty, but at the same time I wasn't going to volunteer more than what was asked of me.

Finally, I sat up and looked down at him. "Should I go?" I asked in a soft tone.

He looked up at me and brushed loose strands of hair behind my ear. "No, but if I asked... could you cut the others loose and only be mine to play with?" he asked.

I could have said a number of things; I knew one thing for certain, I wasn't interested in a relationship. I wasn't ready. I also knew that any commitment, even one as simple as being a solitary play-toy for someone fell into the "relationship" category. I simply asked him, "Why?"

One of the hazards in the kind of playing I was doing was that sometimes the other person ends up falling for you.

> *Whore Tip: If your playmate begins to get emotion-*
> *ally involved, break it off. No matter what they tell*
> *you, they cannot play this game by your rules anymore.*

It would have thrown me off to find out Mark was becoming attached. Every conversation we had revolved around sexual acts, specifically what he wanted to do to me and how he wanted me to act. If he got mushy on me, I would have to rethink my instincts.

"I don't want to share you," he said never taking his eyes off of me. "You should only be serving me," asserting his desire to be the top.

Being Mark's fantasy of a submissive had led to a lot of moans and wetness on my part, but I knew that this wasn't a long-term thing that I had any interest in pursuing. I am not a submissive personality, quite the opposite. This little romp into his world was a fun vacation, but I didn't want to live there.

I decided the best way to handle it was blunt honesty. In the back of my mind, it might also be what led me home before the snore fest. One could hope.

I slid out of the covers and walked to the window. I didn't feel vulnerable being naked, it was quite empowering. "I don't want that," I said turning and meeting his gaze. "This is fun, you are fun, but I am not looking for anything serious and being only yours is just that, serious."

I turned back again to face the window and kept my back to him intentionally, making sure that he knew there was a line and his request had crossed it. I also wouldn't end up giggling if the aggressive stud that he portrayed himself to be suddenly became whiney.

I heard him move behind me. I wasn't sure what to expect, but I wasn't going to back down.

He came up behind me and stood close enough that I could feel the warmth of his body but he didn't touch me. I assumed this was his way of making his own stand. We stood there for a moment, and I wasn't sure if he thought I would turn around, but I wasn't going to lose this one, however silly it might be.

"I know you don't want serious," he continued, "that is not what I am saying. I want you to be at my beck and call purely for sex, nothing more."

I knew right then that it wasn't simply a fantasy for Mark. He needed this, to balance some part of his life he was not in control of. He could control our interactions, and he needed more. I was not willing to fill that vacuum for him. I also knew that an overly dramatic scene of walking out would make the effort I had put in to making the night, which should hold many orgasms, for naught. I wasn't going to waste it.

Whore Tip: Never waste a trip. Since there is only one thing you are getting out of it, try to never walk away without that one thing.

I took a deep breath, uncrossed my arms and turned around, placing my hands on his chest. I looked into his eyes and simply said, "I'll think about it," and winked. With that he grabbed me around the waist, turned my body and pushed me onto the bed. Spreading my legs, he held my thighs apart and looked at all of me as he pushed my legs even wider. With as much hunger as the first night, he placed his lips on the moist folds between my legs.

The rest of the day was alternating positions at his request. I was willing to play the game with him to the fullest. He believed I would be what he wanted. It is one of the biggest turn-ons in the world to be just that, a fantasy come to life, and that is what I was for that entire night.

Ok, most of the night. I knew what staying held in store for me. I fell asleep before him, on purpose. It didn't work. The first snore that tore through my dreams felt like the door had just been ripped from its hinges by some beast from a Grimm fairytale. I might be over exaggerating a little bit, but I was awake, again, and this time I wasn't willing to simply lay there listening to the buzz saw and then drive home angry and tired. I did what every self-respecting girl should do: I quietly gathered my clothes, got dressed and left.

As I drove home at three am, I debated texting him and making up an excuse for my departure. I didn't know his number and really, I didn't think he deserved an apology. I let any lingering guilt go, and snuggled into my own bed at home after a hot shower. That was one of the best night's sleep I have ever had.

23

MARRIED MEN ARE ASSHOLES

When I woke up in the morning I wasn't surprised to see that Mark had blown up my phone and email. I had turned it off to sleep. Sneaking out in the middle of the night would usually cause a complete dismissal, and I was kind of hoping to never hear from him again. Instead I had almost a dozen voicemails; in each one he became steadily angrier. I suppose he was justified in a way.

I texted Alex and Baley to see if they wanted to do breakfast. I was hungry, and while I knew I should just ignore the whole thing, I had the feeling Mark wasn't going away that easy. I had taken his control away.

Alex met me at a local diner that is pretty famous for its French toast. Each slice takes up an entire plate and there are roasted almonds on the bottom. The food is always amazing and I can never finish the whole thing, but it's comfort food and that is what I wanted.

I walked in the door and found Alex had beaten me there. She had coffee already on the table and I threw in a couple of sugars and some creamer as the waitress came over to take our orders. When the waitress walked away I simply handed my phone to Alex and let her listen to all of the messages. She only listened to the first and last.

"Wow," she said as she handed the phone back. "Was he any good?" she asked then immediately said, "Don't answer that, I am going to assume he was or this..." she gestured at the phone now sitting on the table next to the silverware, "is definitely not worth it."

I took another swig of the coffee, and said, "I snuck out because his snoring was like being trapped in a lumber mill all night. Not my best move, but I wasn't sure I wouldn't put him out of both of our misery with a pillow if I didn't pull a 'Mission Impossible' type maneuver."

"You realize you're going to have to call him," Alex said as the waitress arrived with the mouthwatering toast of epicness.

I poured my syrup and said, "Technically I don't, because he has never given me his number. I just have his email and IM name." Alex made a face, a cross between a scowl and frown. It was very akin to the face a person makes when they smell something terrible.

"You don't have his number?" she asked, and I could tell her voice was laced with judgment. Although most people wouldn't think about it, judgment has a distinct tone and inflection. Alex had mastered it. This was full frontal judgment.

I took another bite. Not answering wasn't an option and no matter what I said it wouldn't end well for me.

After I swallowed I said, "No, it wasn't important and he is a very private person".

She got the look again and simply asked, "I thought you were not going to do this with married men anymore?"

"He isn't married. He is just...." I couldn't say the rest. I knew she was right. I ate my toast, and felt dumb for not having seen it before.

Whore Tip: When a story seems too much like a movie plot, it probably is.

I debated how I should handle the situation. I wanted to be wrong and for Mark to just be a weirdo. It says something when you want someone to be a weirdo versus a cheater. Weirdos are easier to deal with.

I pulled out my phone and sent Mark a message. "Sorry, something came up. I am up now; give me a call when you can." That was the third version of the message I had typed out. The others were accusatory and full of expletives that apps always wanted to spell-correct for you.

I was driving home from breakfast when he called. I answered, knowing it was him, with a simple "Hello".

' I know you're sorry for your actions." This wasn't going to go well.

"How long have you been married for?" I asked. The gloves were off. I used my nice voice, but I was done. His pause spoke volumes. "A while then?" I added. I heard him take a deep breath. Why people in these types of situations don't just hang up, I will never understand. When someone gets caught in something it has always amazed me that, ninety percent of the time the reaction is to continue to lie, as if that is the smart route to go. The few people who can own up for what they did and take responsibility are way above those that can't. Of course, those that don't get themselves into that type of situation are miles above those.

Whore Tip: You can always heal hurt that is caused by someone, you can never heal betrayal.

"I'm, well, we're getting divorced," he said. Not only had he lied, but that was a terrible excuse. There are, I am sure, many situations where a couple is getting divorced and there is nothing wrong with pursuing other avenues until the divorce is final. If they are not up front about it, regardless of the excuse as to why, is not one of those times where it is okay.

He went on to explain, although I didn't ask, that the divorce was messy and there were two kids involved and a rather nasty issue over custody. She was putting him through the ringer and watching every aspect of his life in order to catch him and take his kids away.

I think he was looking for sympathy. That was a mistake on his part.

> *Whore Tip: It doesn't matter what kind of playmate you have, it is never, never, never a good idea to be with someone who is married. There is no reason that is ever okay. Being the "other woman" just makes you trashy.*

He was waiting for a reaction on my part; actually waiting for me to be okay with the whole arrangement. What he got was nothing close, not any more.

"Lose my number," I said.

"What?" he replied.

I think it's funny when people ask you to repeat something you have said, not because they didn't hear you, but because they are hoping the next time you say it, they'll get a different answer. That wasn't happening.

"Mark, I want you to lose my number." When I said it again I was sure to be very clear, speaking slower so he heard every word.

He started to try to explain things again, ignoring what I said to him, so I hung up. It wasn't worth it. He called back a couple of times. He didn't leave a voicemail until the next day, to tell me he really wanted a chance to explain. I wasn't about to give him that chance.

I found that even though I had been betrayed in the worst ways in my last relationship, I was still very trusting. I think there are parts of your personality that are not as easily broken as others.

Unfortunately, that was the second time I had ended up as part of the betrayal of another. It made me less willing to be "understanding" when things weren't all out in the open. I was taking a different approach to letting things slide, and asserting my own dominance.

24

PLANK

Throughout my adventures, I was constantly looking for new recruits. You never know when a playmate might be only a one-nighter versus an ongoing plaything, so it's a good idea to make sure your dance card is always full.

I met Brandon through MySpace. As much as the advertisements claimed it was for music and musicians, and—don't get me wrong—I found amazing bands and artists I would have otherwise not been exposed to, it was also a great way to meet people and hook-up.

I was checking my emails one night when a new email popped up. It was a younger man, age twenty, asking me if I was into younger guys. Before answering him, I went to his page and went through his pictures. I knew I was into younger guys, but it was dependent on the guy.

Looking through his pictures, which were mostly selfies in the bathroom mirror, he was cute. Tall, brown hair cut shorter, brown eyes and very chiseled abs he didn't mind showing off. While not true for all young men (or women) in their twenties, I have noticed that some are blessed with an easy-to-maintain and nice-to-look-at body that seems like they were designed for pleasing. That and sports.

I decided to email him back with a quick, "Maybe, depends on the guy." He asked for my IM name and on which service. Talking via email can be a pain, but you can ignore an IM or even block a user. I've found it a good way to do some sorting.

Brandon, although very nice to look at, was somewhat difficult to talk to. His literacy, shall we say, was not that great. He would ask me constantly what I was wearing, what I was doing, and did I want to hook up.

It wasn't very appealing. I told the girls about this one and they all thought I should cut him loose. There was a lot of giggling and they insisted on seeing his picture before making the call that he needed to go the way of many of my other would be suitors.

The next time he sent me a message, I told him that I had a boyfriend and needed to stop messaging him. This wasn't exactly truthful, but I couldn't bring myself to tell him that the problem was that he was dumb and talking to him was lowering my IQ. According to Sally, that would be mean. At least someone is my conscience.

> *Whore Tip: If someone has a trait that you don't find endearing or attractive, don't think that everyone feels the way you do. Now, if the person is being mean or hurtful, feel free to point that out in the same tone they are using.*

Life continued as normal, and about two months passed, when I got an email from Brandon. It simply said, "I'm Board." I had to look at it a couple of times to make sure I was reading it correctly.

"You're a plank of wood?" I responded after a couple of minutes.

He sent me back a smiley face with a "?". He was really dumb.

I wanted to clarify, so that he understood the difference between 'Bored' and 'Board', but it seemed pointless. I started calling him "Plank". It seemed fitting.

*Whore Tip: Stupid is never sexy, naive is sexy. If you
are dumb, it is best you just stand there and look pretty.*

The following is how the conversation played out. I am warning
you, it is not for the grammar police.

PLANK: Im horny and my pants have a huge boner in them now.

ME: How did that happen?

PLANK: Cuz I was thinking of me and you.

ME: Really? What were you thinking?

PLANK: That we should do it.

ME: Do what?

PLANK: U now

ME: ?

PLANK: U now, like hook up. (*now = know, took me twice*)

ME: Hook up to what?

PLANK: U

ME: ?

PLANK: U shood hook up w/me.

ME: Where should this magical hook-up happen?

PLANK: Ur place. I live with dad.

ME: Since we have never actually met, I don't feel safe with you
just coming over to "hook-up".

PLANK: Wanna meat?

ME: Um (*I really wanted to ask if he was taking me out for a steak
dinner. Probably not.*)

PLANK: U afraid?

ME: Of what?

PLANK: Meating me

ME: No (*At this point I was terrified of his inability to type
small words.*)

PLANK: So u wanna meat me?

ME: I am supposed to hang out with friends tonight. What were
you thinking? (*Yes, I felt a little bad for the guy.*)

PLANK: I dunno, like we could just hang out for a min, U can see if I am scary.

ME: Ok, let me see what I can do.

I copied this entire message strand into an email with the subject line "Meet Plank" and sent it to Alex and Sally. Then I called them to hear their reactions.

Alex: What the hell? Is this real?

Sally: Did he go to school?

There was a lot of laughing, and jokes made about his meat. I told the girls I felt obligated to meet him. I said he had to be the best kisser in the world, because he had to have been given something as a gift, since it hadn't been being blessed with an average intelligence.

The girls reluctantly agreed. I think they knew I was going to do it anyway. I told them I had made up an excuse that I was hanging out with friends, and as a reward for going with me I would buy them coffee and pie from a local twenty-four hour restaurant that served some of the best pie around. With the enticement of food they agreed.

Back in IM:

ME: Back

PLANK: Hey sexy

ME: So, I can meet up with you for a couple of mins if you like, to see if we have a connection.

PLANK: Ok. Like for how long.

ME: 15 mins

PLANK: Why?

ME: I told you I was hanging out with friends. Up to you, do you want to meet or not?

PLANK: Yes. Where?

I found out he lived about twenty minutes south of where I did, and we agreed to meet up in the parking lot of an ice cream shop that was about the same distance for both of us. It was also a public place and therefore less creepy than a dark street.

I asked Sally to drive so he wouldn't see my car. She agreed, being the ever so cautious friend, but again tried to talk me out of it. I, however, was on a mission and had to see if he spoke the same way he typed. Maybe he was just bad at using a computer. I knew that probably wasn't the case, but I was willing to give it a shot.

When we pulled up, he was already there. He had told me he drove a black mustang. He did, but it looked like he was in the middle of working on it, as one of the fenders had been replaced and was a primer grey. He was leaning against his car when we pulled up.

Plank was wearing basketball shorts and a T-shirt. He had on flip-flops, too. While we do live in the sunny state of Florida, and the summer can be really hot, there is no excuse for not making an attempt at a good first impression. I started to tell Sally to drive off, but he spotted us.

"There's a real winner," Alex said as he started to walk up to the car. I got out. He smiled when he saw me. He had a really cute smile and I was lost in it for about three seconds.

Then he said, "Damn girl, you fine." I didn't think I would ever hear that phrase outside of a rap video or a club.

Whore Tip: Trust your loins. If they are screaming run, then run. Even girls can go limp.

I introduced Alex and Sally, using fake names I thought of right then. No fair, dragging them into this. He asked if I wanted to talk in his car for a minute. He wanted to show me his stereo. I am not sure why guys think that seeing a stereo will make a girl's panties drop, it won't.

I nodded and headed toward his car, as Alex yelled, "You two kids don't do anything I wouldn't do." This made Plank laugh. He didn't know that Alex would have done nothing with him, so we were already breaking her proclamation.

I got in his car and he turned it on, turned up the stereo, leaned over to me and pushing his lips against mine began to suck on my face. He was all lips and tongue, and it wasn't confined to my lips or mouth. I felt like he was licking the last crumbs on earth off of my face right before he was going to eat me. Then his hands were on my legs and breasts like a rabid octopus.

I pulled back and pushed him away, wiping my face off. "Wait" I said, trying to get my breath.

"I thought you wanted me, baby," he said as he leaned back, I think trying to sound seductive. He had a raging hard-on. I am sorry, a 'boner', that I could see standing up in his shorts.

"Actually, I wanted to meet you. See if we clicked. You almost just ate my face," I said, still wiping the wetness off.

I think he realized that I was about to get out of the car when he said, "Sorry baby, you are just so hot. One more try... please?" The please was elongated and he did a kind of pouty face, sticking out his lower lip.

This didn't do a thing for me, but I was in a giving mood. "One more kiss and it better be amazing."

He nodded and leaned in. The kiss started off gentle and had some potential for about ten seconds, and then he started to engulf my face again. I pushed him off, and said, "I am sorry Plank, I mean Brandon, I've got to run. My friends are waiting," and opened the car door. He tried to talk me into staying, but I closed the door and walked as quickly as I could back to Sally's car, wiping my face again. I got in and simply said, "Drive."

I explained what had happened to the girls over the promised pie and coffee. Alex made me repeat the part where I called him "Plank" to his face. Even the third time I told her, it brought fits of laughter.

Over the next several days, which turned into weeks and then a month, Plank would IM me. I hadn't given him my phone number so that was his only way of contacting me. In his messages, he went into great detail about how horny he was and what a huge boner he had. His words, not mine. He kept trying to tell me how he could make all my fantasies come true.

Once, I decided to reply. I had a couple of glasses of wine in me, and I asked what fantasies he thought he would be suited to fulfill. He told me he didn't have a suit.

That was the last time I answered him. I hope he was able to find someone who thought he was as amazing as he thought he was. I also hope, if he did, that they never reproduce.

25

YOU SAY HE IS
"JUST A FRIEND"

For most of my adult life, I have played on-line games, most of them fantasy based. Elves and dragons, not the other kind. Geesh. It is the Nerdy Girl side of me, and I have met many fun and interesting people online. These types of games are set up for social interaction. Can't kill the big monster on your own? Ask someone for help.

This type of entertainment isn't for everyone, but it is an industry that generates *billions* annually so there must be at least a few other nerds out there who agree with me.

I was playing one night with several others in a group and we were navigating an especially difficult dungeon. We were losing more than we were winning. One of the people in this group of foolhardy heroes was a mage (a person who uses magic to fight) called Mestrom.

His real name is Jared. Now, before you jump to any opinions about talking to people online in games you have never met before, keep in mind it is not any different than any online dating site, with the exception of being able to send a lightning bolt through a giant spider instead of reading a plethora of online questionnaires about "What are the six things you can't live without" where most people only seem to give their phone as number one.

Jared was very funny, and when I logged in (nerd speak for going online to play a game) he became a person I looked forward to playing with.

> *Whore Tip: A good sense of humor and charm are always sexier than a nice tight ass. At least when someone has a sense of humor, they know how to use it.*

There are many resources for gamers that allow voice chat over the computer. That is how my playtime with Jared really started.

At first it was in game, and only when I was playing. Then I found myself chatting with him when I had logged out and was simply sitting in front of my computer doing nothing.

Eventually he offered up his 'digits' and we began texting and calling each other. He was smart, funny and sweet. Not what I was looking for in a playmate. I wasn't interested in talking to my play-mates as much as I was Jared. Conversation wasn't necessary to achieve my end game with a playmate. In this case it didn't matter, because Jared lived in Missouri.

Missouri is jokingly called the "show me" state, and this led to many a teasing reference by me. The third time Jared and I spoke on the phone; he asked me if I would be willing to send him a picture. He wanted to see if I looked the way I had described myself.

Anyone who has ever done any kind of online interactions will tell you there is a lot of false advertising, or bait-and-switch, when it comes to what a person looks like in reality. You almost never see a person post an unflattering picture of themselves, and when they do you have to question if they believed posting a terrible picture was to say, "Hey I am a real person and comfortable with myself", or "I'm an idiot that doesn't know how this whole dating thing works". Most of the time, I am convinced it is the latter.

Whore Tip: Always use a flattering picture of yourself and avoid "selfies" at all costs. A selfie is the best way to say, "I practice taking good pictures of myself because I have no friends to take photos of me".

Because I am such a generous person, I was more than willing to send a picture or two of myself. I made sure he wasn't expecting them, so I sent them from my phone in the middle of a work day. He worked construction during the day, so he was rarely near his phone. It seemed that he was on a break at the exact time I hit send, because it took exactly sixty seconds for him to respond with: "WOW!".

I smiled when I read the text, but I didn't reply until later. Jared was still in the friend/flirty zone. If he had been closer, I would have taken a different path with our interactions, but being several states away afforded me the ability to have him in the category "fun to talk with".

When I got home I was about to text him a reply to the "WOW", when he sent me a picture of himself. It was a picture of a real picture. He said that he figured I wanted an actual picture and not a selfie. He was correct, but his solution was a bit different. The picture though, spoke volumes. He was an Italian Stallion and looked every bit what you would hope to find on a Vespa trip through Rome.

He had jet black hair that was just above his shoulders, and he had a mustache and goatee in the picture. He had an amazing smile with dimples, and dark brown eyes that were the color of coffee with just a hint of cream in it. This, against his olive complexion, surprised me.

He was a NERD in the truest sense of the word.

Don't get me wrong, I am also a nerd, but on the whole I have found nerds to be people who are slightly awkward in some way. For instance, I am six-feet tall which, since I was twelve when I hit that height, made some parts of my life more difficult I think than a girl who was five-foot-four to five-foot-six.

When we spoke that night, I decided to find out more about my now much-sexier-than-I-first-thought friend.

He was six-foot-three, and said he had broad shoulders. Jared told me that he didn't consider himself well built, but stocky. He made a point of telling me that he had been fat, had worked hard to lose the weight, and his job had helped a lot. He worked outside and was constantly moving around doing hard labor.

A part of me was disappointed that we had not been able to meet under different circumstances, as in being able to set him up as one of my playmates. In the same breath I enjoyed talking with him and we had similar interests. I had found a genuine friend and unless I started a relationship with him that line could not be crossed.

> *Whore Tip: Remember that a FWB (Friend with Benefits) is never actually supposed to be a real friend. Even with "just a friend", an emotional attachment can occur and the last thing you ever need with a playmate is emotions.*

Over the next couple of weeks, we began to speak about our past relationships. Jared was curious as to why I was single. He actually asked me, "What is wrong with you?" I made him laugh by telling him that I thought it was my obsession with chewing my own toenails that might be keeping the men at bay. I got one of those obligatory, yet terrified, laughs a person will give you when they are not sure if what you said was true, and a huge part of them is hoping you follow the statement up with "just kidding". I actually let it hang there for a couple minutes, before I told him I was messing with him. His sigh of relief was audible.

He told me his last relationship ended similarly to mine. The girl he was with cheated on him. His ex went so far as to move her new man into their house under the guise of letting her friend stay with them while he found an apartment. When Jared caught them in bed together, instead of acting shocked or apologizing, his ex asked Jared to join the activities.

Jared told me he had always had the fantasy of being in a three-some. Most guys do, I think it's part of their DNA. The ones that don't are a little creepy to me. This hadn't been the type of three-some most guys, including Jared, imagine. Most men fantasize about two girls being involved, and not having it start by walking in on your girlfriend cheating on you. That relationship ended and he was forced to move rather quickly.

I told Jared my story about the end of my last relationship, and he of course could sympathize. He asked me if I was going to start dating again.

> *Whore Tip: It is dangerous territory when anyone asks a person with playmates about dating. For the record, Dating = Relationship. Tread lightly when venturing into this minefield.*

The question backed me into a corner, unfortunately of my own design. It was the first time someone other than my previously mentioned friends, or those men I decided to possibly make into play-mates, had opened that can of worms.

I simply answered, "I don't know," and then made up an excuse about having to run and hung up the phone. I didn't handle it well, and I didn't immediately understand why.

I was completely comfortable with what I was doing and didn't really care what people thought of me, but for some reason talking about it with Jared made me uncomfortable. I needed to figure out why before I spoke to him again. It may seem silly, but I got the feeling he wasn't done asking me questions.

It was very easy for me to be comfortable in the world I had constructed, controlling those who were in my world with me. In talking with Jared, I realized that I was the one in total control of who went in and out of my adventure, and I wasn't as comfortable as I thought letting everyone in.

26

How To Make "The Switch"

I did my best to avoid Jared without seeming to avoid him. I would go online and play the game and make sure we were always in a large group. I would text him, but when he called, I wouldn't answer. He asked when I could chat again, I told him that I was in the middle of a project at work and it was taking a lot out of me. He said he understood, and that whenever I had time, he would love to chat.

"What the hell is wrong with me?" I asked a couple of days later at a coffee meet-up. Alex smirked and took a sip, obviously being unwilling to be the first to answer that one.

I had told the girls all about Jared and what had happened. Sally asked if he was relationship material. I told her I didn't know, that I hadn't thought about it. This was not the whole truth. I figured that might be at the core of the whole problem, but I wasn't willing to deal with it yet.

"So you're not sleeping with him?" Baley asked. Both Alex and I looked over at her.

"Were you asleep at the part where she said he lived in Missouri?" Alex asked.

"Yes," Baley said sticking her tongue out at Alex. "I meant; she could be having phone sex with him or video chat sex. There are ways to do naughty things without being in the room together."

"This is true," I said, nodding at Baley. I watched a little scowl play across Alex's face out of the corner of my eye.

> *Whore Tip: Video chat can be amazing to do naughty things with someone who is not able to be next to, or on top of you, just then, but remember that everything can be recorded. Video chat sex can easily turn into amateur porn. You don't want to have a secretly taped video of your playtime forwarded to you by your mom.*

Taking another sip, I said, "I think I should just tell him. I mean, we're friends, and I am not ashamed. I think if he can't handle the truth then that is his problem, not mine." By the time the words left my lips, I felt confident in them. This was my choice and why did I care what some guy I just met a couple of months ago and lived in Missouri thought about it?

"Or you could just add him to your roster and do the video sex thing," Alex said with a shit-eating grin on her face.

Sally looked over and gently slapped her on the arm. "Knock it off, Bitchy-Mc-Bitcherson." We all laughed and poor Baley spit out the latte she had just taken a sip of.

The consensus of the girls was that I should just tell him where I was at and let the cards fall where they may. If he was to remain a friend he should be able to be understanding of those parts of me that might not be the same choices he would make.

I texted him on the way back from coffee and asked, "Are you up for a chat tonight?"

Jared responded almost immediately: "Yes! When?"

I texted back: "In an hour."

"I'll be waiting 😊".

An hour would give me enough time to get a couple of glasses of wine in me. Not enough to get me drunk, but some liquid courage to get me started. Even though it was the right thing to do in telling him, that didn't mean that it was an easy thing.

Two glasses of my favorite red and getting into my comfy clothes, pajama pants and a cami tank top; I sat on the couch and dialed the phone. After five rings, just as I thought it might go to voicemail, he picked up.

"Hello, beautiful." His voice sounded breathy.

"Hi, sweetie. Why are you out of breath?"

"Honestly, it's silly. I was in another room when I heard the phone ring. I ran to grab it and tripped over the table when jumping up and needless to say, it took way more than it should have to reach the phone," he said.

I laughed.

"I hope everything is okay, you have been kind of avoiding me," he said.

"You're right. I am sorry."

"Did I do something wrong?"

I hesitated. "No. Actually, you just asked me something I wasn't prepared to answer, it ... well.... um... How are you?" I asked, stalling.

"I am... wait... you just changed the subject. What is it? I don't want things to be weird between us."

I took a deep breath. "You asked me when I would be ready for another relationship."

"I am sorry... I didn't mean to..."

"Stop, it isn't you." I sighed. "I don't want a *relationship* right now. I, well, I have a specific type of relationships and I thought it was better to try to explain. So let me just explain, and then at the end you can hang up and never speak to me again, or I'll answer any questions you still have."

"Did you say relationships? Plural?" he asked.

I knew what he was thinking immediately, and wanted to take back my horrible wording. I had just hit the nerve from his last heartbreak. Maybe sliding into that third glass of wine hadn't been the best choice.

I dove right into my explanation of how I had decided I wanted playmates and that I wasn't ready for anything with an emotional attachment. He gave me little "okays" every now and then to let me know he was listening. He seemed to be giving me time to explain. It was very nice because, as I was explaining it, I recognized that the whole plan sounded much better when I had discussed it with the girls over coffee.

It was easy to tell potential playmates because when I talked, texted or emailed with them, I would just say, "I am not looking for a relationship, just a fuck buddy." This needed no further explanation. With Jared, I had to explain from the beginning: how I decided to take this route, how I went about it and where I was at with it. By the time I figured I should stop talking, I was surprised he hadn't hung up the phone. If the roles had been reversed, I would have hung up the phone when the words "multiple playmates at the same time" were said.

"So, that's it," I said.

"Interesting."

I wasn't prepared for "interesting". I was ready to have him think I was a slut, or that I was running away from my issues, or any number of things, but "interesting" wasn't one of them. I didn't know how to respond.

"Interesting?"

"Yes, interesting," he said.

"Okay."

I was at a total loss, and long pauses between everything being said only made it worse. I thought of telling him that I had to run, but I needed to see where this was going.

"Can I be a playmate?" Jared asked.

"What?"

"I have wanted to fuck you since the moment I saw your picture. So, can I be added to your list?"

"I... umm... What?"

"Randi, I am not trying to be too forward, but I figure you would appreciate the honesty, and really this is the easiest way to ask you. Can we play together?"

What the hell? Just WHAT?! My mind screamed. An incredibly handsome guy, instead of dumping our newly formed friendship, tells me he wants to play. I wasn't sure if it was a good idea, but when he said he wanted to fuck me, I started to get wet. I did the only thing I could do, I went for it.

"What did you have in mind, Jared?"

"What are you wearing? Wait, it doesn't matter. I want you to go to your room and take it off and lay on the bed... do that for me please?"

"Okay."

I was hesitant. I wasn't sure if it was a good idea. But there I was, heading into my bedroom. I did as he asked, stripped off my clothes and lay across my bed sideways, letting myself stretch out. I guess I had known it would be a possibility that Jared would get turned on by the explanation of my exploits. I should be happy, in a way, that he hadn't simply masturbated during my tale of naughtiness. I hadn't given a lot of details, but I had explained that I got what I wanted by being a fantasy for some of the men. I picked up the phone and my voice switched into more of a breathy whisper.

"As requested," I breathed.

"God, you're so fucking hot. I am so hard right now."

"What are you wearing?" I asked.

"I can take it all off..."

"I didn't ask that. I asked what you were wearing?" I repeated.

"Jeans and a T-shirt"

"Is your hard cock pressing up against the jeans?"

"Yes"

"I want you to feel the tightness with each throb; I want you to feel how much you want me."

"God, I want you," he said, his voice catching.

"What do you want first?"

"I... I've never..."

"Tell me what you want," I said.

> *Whore Tip: Being able to have enough control of a situation to give control to your partner, gently guiding them, can lead to one of the biggest turn-ons ever for them.*

"I wanna taste you."

I moaned.

"God, Randi."

"Jared... tell me what you want me to do." I moaned again. "I am so tight as I slide my fingers into my wet pussy. I want your lips on me, Jared."

"Let me take it out, please, I want to touch myself," he said, his voice rough.

"Yes... Please..."

I heard the rustling of clothes though the phone as he freed himself from the confines of his jeans. I closed my eyes and pictured his face between my legs, him looking up at me; his mouth covered in a sheen of my wetness. I was close.

"Are you touching yourself?" I asked.

"Yes."

"Tell me what you want," I insisted.

"I want to kiss up your thighs. I want to feel the heat of your pussy."

"More," I breathed out with a whimper. I was so close. I tried to not be too loud; I didn't want him to stop.

"I want to take my tongue and lick the sides of your lips, until they part and my tongue touches your clit. I want to taste how wet you are for me."

"Jared! Yes! Oh, God, Yes!" I screamed as I climaxed.

I almost dropped the phone when I heard him cum. I rode out my orgasm listening to his moans and growls. The release was the perfect thing to break the stress of telling him. For a couple of minutes it was just the sound of both of us letting our breathing return to normal.

"You are as beautiful as you are dangerous," he said.

"You, handsome, have no idea. Goodnight, sexy."

With that, I hung up the phone. If anything else had been said, it would cross the line. If he was going to be a playmate, I needed to make sure the friendship didn't get any more blurred then it already was.

27

YOU FIRST

Keeping the line from blurring with Jared didn't turn out to be as hard as I thought it would be. Although we would make naughty little comments while we were playing in the game, he respected the boundaries I set out the day after our first play session.

> *Whore Tip: Adding long distance playmates can be amazing, especially if you travel a lot. Having a place to dock your ship at each port of call ensures always having an amazing voyage.*

Jared and I played at least once a week. I still was maintaining some regular players on my roster like Brief Intermission, but playing with Jared over the phone let me be creative sexually in different ways.

During the second month, I started playing with toys during our phone encounters. I would let him tell me what he wanted me to be wearing or doing, and even though he couldn't technically see me and he would have no idea if I was or wasn't fulfilling my end of the deal, I always did. Being honest was always the easiest route.

At the beginning of the third month, after a particularly naughty call where Jared asked if I was willing to penetrate myself in more than one opening, he asked if I was willing to send him pictures of a more naked nature.

Pictures to me have always been a little bit dangerous. Once you send them out they can easily become public property.

> *Whore Tip: Any picture that you send out of you in any state of undress should not involve your face, recognizable tattoos, a mirror or a background that can be recognized.*

I felt that Jared was trustworthy, but I am also a fairly trusting person by nature, so I told him that I had to think on it. I could tell he was disappointed, but I knew he would respect my wishes. He enjoyed our playtime, and with each call was getting more and more into the experience.

The next day, while I was at work, I got a text message from Jared. I was in a meeting discussing a new project with several other people. I looked up to see that the slideshow presentation was far from ending, so I opened my messages with the hope he had said something that would pull me out of the boredom of the meeting.

What greeted me was a message that said: "I'll go first, I was thinking about you today." This was accompanied by a picture of the largest penis I had ever seen. I gasped out loud and quickly placed my phone screen-down on the table. Shelly, a coworker, asked me if I was okay. I wasn't. I just nodded to her. After a few seconds, the attention from my minor distraction finally fell away and I made a mental note to never open text messages in meetings again.

After the longest forty-five minutes of my life, I was able to rush out of the meeting and to my office. I was lucky; I worked in an office with walls instead of a cubicle. It was not the type of picture you looked at in a cubicle if you wanted to keep your job.

I opened the text message again and stared at the picture. My jaw dropped.

The picture was taken in the shower, or just after. There were still water droplets everywhere. His shaft stood at attention from his body and it was perfectly straight. The head was a deeper shade of pink than the length of him. You could still see the light olive tint to his skin which made the tip almost a mauve color.

My panties were soaked. I needed a release. I looked at the clock; I had another two hours before I could leave work. I took the phone, slid it in my pants pocket and walked to the bathroom.

As I entered, I glanced under the stalls to see if there was anyone else in the room. There wasn't. That didn't mean someone couldn't walk in at any moment. A chill of excitement ran through me at the thought. It was the first time I had even contemplated being naughty at work. Some people have a fantasy of being bent over the desk at work, but I hadn't really thought about it.

Whore Tip: Never dip your pen in the company inkwell. Sleeping with coworkers always ends badly.

I slid into the largest stall at the end of the row. I unbuttoned my pants, and unzipped them without letting them fall, then undid the bottom buttons of my fitted shirt. I had to wear business attire to work, which usually meant button-down shirts and slacks. Sometimes, we even had to wear suits. I was thankful that this wasn't one of those days.

I used my back to anchor the pants so that anyone looking for an empty stall would not see my pants down around my ankles facing the wrong direction.

I opened the picture again, taking it in. I slid my fingers into my panties, feeling my moist cleft. I was so wet. I started to rub my folds, absorbing the sensation of just letting my fingers stimulate me. My clit was almost vibrating. I couldn't look away from the cock in front of me. I imagined that girth pushing into me, stretching me, feeling the slight pain of him taking me. As I got closer to my climax, I knew that if he had been there with me, he wouldn't hold back. He would have been waiting so long he wouldn't be able to restrain himself. He would push deeper. I had to bite my lip to keep from screaming out. I came hard.

My legs were shaking so badly I was almost unable to continue to stand. I reached out and placed my hand on the opposite wall to steady myself. Just then, I heard another toilet flush in the row and it snapped me back to where I was. I didn't know how loud I had been, even though I had tried to be discreet.

I closed the picture and sent a quick text that simply said, "Thank You," put my phone back in my pocket and cleaned up as best I could. My panties were still very wet, but so was I, so taking them off wasn't an option. I waited, listening until it seemed I was alone. I checked under the stalls to make sure that I was. When I left the stall and washed my hands I made sure I didn't look on the outside how I felt on the inside. I was flushed, but that would be ok. I could just say that I was rushing about if anyone asked.

When I got in my car to drive home I sent Alex the picture and then called. When she picked up, all she said was, "What the hell is that thing?!" I laughed.

In case you were wondering, I didn't have a problem sharing this picture with a friend, because Jared wasn't a significant other. When you are with someone in a relationship, you shouldn't share the intimacy with your friends. If you are with someone to play around, then they are fair game to share, except sexually.

> *Whore Tip: Boyfriends and spouses are always off limits. So are playmates. Unless you are doing a threesome (or foursome), sleeping with your friend's play toy is just tacky and makes you seem desperate.*

Alex asked me exactly how big the "giant member" she was now staring at was. I honestly didn't know. I hadn't expected him to send me a picture of his "cash-and-prizes" so I would have to ask. She said that it looked painful. I voiced that I hoped it was, in a good way. She laughed and told me to call her and let her know when I had the measurements.

When I got home Jared had sent a text: "You are welcome, beautiful." I would like to say I figured out a way to ask subtly about the actual size, but like a kid with a new toy I needed to know right away. If I demanded details, he would give them to me, but I felt that since he had been willing to share, I could give him a little something in return.

Most of the men I had spoken with throughout this time were more than willing to share pictures of their fully-erect penises. Maybe they believed in some weird way they were snake charmers and the sight of their magnificent cocks would make me want to drop my pants. That was not the case, but it did lead me to dismiss a few candidates for lacking proper qualifications.

One of the last encounters we had, Jared asked me to wear a lacy black thong without a bra. I undressed, found the thong and a pair of black heels and put them on. I lay on my stomach on the bed, bent my knees, crossing my legs and moved my hair so it cascaded down my back. Lifting myself up on my elbow I took a picture over my shoulder at an angle. It took a few tries, turning on and off lights and lamps around the room and the closet, to get the perfect shadowing.

I ended up with a picture of part of my back, my round ass and my long legs in heels. Even I was a little impressed with my selfie.

I sent the picture with a note, "Tit for tat. Or in this case: ass for dick", and waited. I knew it wouldn't be long before the phone would ring. It took less than two minutes.

"Hello?" I said, trying to sound more innocent than I had been in a long time.

"What are you trying to do to me?" he asked, his voice a harsh whisper.

Right before I asked him what the hell he was talking about, he followed up with, "I am at a friend's house hanging out, playing a game, and I open my phone to see your amazing ass staring back at me. I started to get hard right there. I had to rush into the bathroom."

I had to laugh.

"Stop laughing, it's not funny." His voice betrayed his humor.

"Why don't you call me when you get home, hot stuff, I got a question for you," I said, giggling. I was willing to let my curiosity wait.

"Are you still wearing the thong?"

"Yes, and nothing else but the heels."

"Oh, God. Randi, do you have any idea what you do to me?"

"Yep"

"Dangerous," he said.

"Very."

"I'll call you back in fifteen."

"Can't wait," I said, and hung up.

I had planned on jumping in the shower when I got home after my work outburst, but after talking to Jared, I thought it might be a good idea to wait. It was twelve minutes before he called.

"I want to take you from behind."

"Do you want me on my knees or bent over?"

"Knees! And I want my hands on your hips," he said.

"I want to thrust my hips back in to you. I want you deep inside me."

"Yes baby, so deep."

"So wet, so tight. I'm beginning to cum around your cock, can you feel me pulse around you as my wetness surrounds you."

"I'm cumming, baby," he groaned.

"Cum for me," I screamed.

"Ohhhh God!!!"

There was silence as we both caught our breath. After a couple of minutes of telling me how amazing I was, he asked what my question was.

I explained that I was curious how big *it* was, exactly. I thought he would find my question cute, or even funny, but he got very quiet.

"What's wrong?" I asked.

"Um... Well..."

"That is your cock right?"

Jared laughed. "Yes, it is mine."

"Then how big is it?"

(silence)

"How is this a bad question?" I asked my voice soft.

"It is big."

"I noticed this. How big?"

Jared sighed on the phone. "I don't know the measurements"

"Never measured the giant, huh? Can you send another picture with an item that is comparable? Like a soda can?"

He laughed again. "I can do that."

"I'll be waiting."

I hung up the phone with a little apprehension. I wasn't sure why he had reacted so weirdly to the question. He didn't have a reason to be ashamed. I decided to jump in the shower and let the hot water wash away the weirdness of the phone call, along with the evidence of my two separate orgasmic adventures.

28

BABY'S ARM
HOLDING AN APPLE

I stayed in the shower until the hot water ran out, enjoying the relaxation of the steam and letting myself take a moment to be happy. I thought about my ex and realized that the pain and hurt was just a dull ache. I was doing exactly what I wanted to do, and with who I wanted to do it with. It was an amazing accomplishment from just a few months previous.

I got out of the shower, and wrapping my hair and body in towels, I walked into my room to check my phone. There were four messages from Jared.

#1: I am sorry I was weird. I just don't want to stop being able to play.

#2: I have had girls turn me down before.

#3: Call me after, please, either way.

I was back to being anxious. Men can be weird sometimes, and what the hell did "I have had girls turn me down before" mean? I decided to bite the bullet and look at text #4. It was two pictures, one from the side and one from the top looking down. I dropped the phone and paced around the room for a minute before picking it up again.

He was HUGE.

Not just large, HUGE. He had an item in the picture to compare with it. It was a soda can. He must have taken my idea. The can was dwarfed by his manhood.

Just for the record, a standard soda can is about five inches tall and two and a half inches at the widest point. I measured. He was easily almost double the size of the can.

I didn't know how to react. I could see why he was freaked out by my question. It hadn't occurred to me that he might have a reason that our type of arrangement had been working for him.

Looking at the pictures again, I knew I wouldn't even be able to touch my thumb and forefinger together if I was holding it. He had asked me to call, but I didn't know what to say. I almost sent Alex the picture, but I knew I couldn't handle what she would say right then. It was almost comical, but I knew from the way Jared had reacted that this was a very sore point with him. I couldn't help it: I giggled a little when I thought of his previous girls and how sore they must have been.

I got dressed and grabbed a snack and glass of water. This allowed me a little time to figure out what exactly I was going to say.

When I dialed the phone, he picked up before it even rang.

"Hiya, handsome," I said.

"You called."

"Of course silly, you asked me to."

"I wasn't sure you would," Jared said.

"Ye of little faith."

"Very funny. What did you think?"

"Honestly?" I hesitated.

"Please."

"It is huge."

"I know," he said without any smugness or pride. He explained that when he got with women and made it into the bedroom, when he "whipped it out", they would often refuse.

A few times he had lovers attempt to have sex with him and he wouldn't fit. He had never had anal for that reason. Anal was off the table with a dick that size. No amount of lube would allow that penetration.

Then he stunned me for a third time that day with eight simple words:

"I want to come down and see you."

It was more than I could mentally take that day, and I went into shock. His voice was there, but I couldn't make out what he was saying. Then I heard him repeating my name, "Randi, you there? You okay? Hello? Randi, answer me!"

"Yeah. Hi," I finally replied.

"I am sorry, I shouldn't have asked. I understand. Goodnight, Beautiful," he said and hung up.

Texting the girls to go out dancing and drinking that Friday night was sheer instinct. It was Wednesday, and Friday seemed a million miles away. I didn't call or text Jared for a couple of days. I stayed off the game as well. Unlike telling him about my current relationship preferences, his coming to see me would take whatever it was we had to a different level.

When Friday night finally arrived, I was the first stop on the round up. Sally, our token designated driver that night, asked "Are you Okay?" when she saw my face.

> *Whore Tip: Drinking with your friends is acceptable. Getting shit-faced at home alone is a recipe for disaster. Drinking only enhances emotions, and loneliness or sadness should never be enhanced.*

"I will be," I replied. Sally let it go, and we sped away to round up our other partners in crime.

We arrived at a restaurant and got a pager, which Alex handed to me, to notify us when our table was ready. I went to sit on a bench outside. The evening was a pleasant one, which couldn't always be said living in Florida. Alex and Baley sat beside me letting Sally and Lucy stand.

"So, what is on your mind Randi?" Lucy said.

"I have a problem," I started. "Remember I told you about Jared?"

They all nodded. I went on to explain the entire situation from beginning to end; what our interactions were in the beginning, what they grew into, and what he was asking now. I also included the pictures. That part took the longest, because the girls had to go through the same band of emotions I had.

It was finally Baley that said, "I think you should meet him. He has been nothing but respectful of your rules."

Sally and Lucy both agreed. "I think you probably have him going nuts wondering if you are ever going to call him again. How many days has it been?" Alex asked.

"Today makes three," I said not feeling great about my choices that week.

"You wanted to experience this whole thing, and it isn't scripted you know. Give him a shot," Sally chimed in.

"Who knows if that Goliath is even going to fit?" said Lucy.

Alex gestured with her arms wide apart and made a horrified face.

"Plus, he might be amazing at oral," Baley added. The plastic pager went off and we moved inside.

The night was fun. We had an amazing dinner and then went to Bricktown 54 to dance, which we did for hours. My favorite handsome bartender was there, and I was able to flirt carefree and score us a few rounds.

I was returning to the table with what we swore was our final round of drinks, when I heard someone call my name over the music. I turned to see The Pilot standing there with Toad, waving me over.

I just shook my head 'no' and went back to the high-top where the girls were waiting.

"The Pilot is here," I said, as I passed out the drinks.

"Where?" Lucy asked and Alex shook her head.

Lucy didn't have to wonder for long. My refusal to go to his table apparently meant he should walk over to mine. I took a sip of my drink, surprised he even remembered my name.

"Hey Ladies," he said as he walked up.

I was forming a nice, but not so nice retort for him when Alex blurted out, "Yeah, no. We're going to pass."

"What?" he said. Gauging his level of drunkenness, I don't think he was able to comprehend what she was saying.

"Go away. We are not interested," Alex said, indicating all of us. He still didn't get the hint.

"Bottoms up, I guess this is last call," I said and swallowed the last of my drink. The other girls did the same and ignoring The Pilot's lame questions, we left the club. He followed us until we got to the door. We told the bouncer, who made me look tiny, that The Pilot was being a creep and following us and we made our escape.

Alex and Baley needed to be up fairly early the next day, so we called it a night. When Sally dropped me at home, I stripped off my club clothes in favor of my PJs and got a glass of water. Always hydrate after a night of drinking.

I reached for my phone, and against what would have been the sober me's better judgment, I called Jared.

"Hello," he sounded sleepy.

"Hi," I said. "I know it is late, but I wanted to say I am sorry for being such a bitch and I would love to see you in person. So let me know if you still want to see me."

"What?" he said.

"Just call me tomorrow, sexy," I said and hung up. Another shining example of why you should not call or text when you are drunk.

I woke up the next day with my phone going off somewhere in my covers. It took me a minute to find it. It was a text from Jared telling me to check my email.

I did and saw an itinerary for one Jared Basciano flying into Tampa the next Friday night at 8:00 pm. I read the email twice.

29

LARGER THAN LIFE

Friday arrived before I could come to terms with what was about to happen. After talking it over with the girls, I decided not to rent a hotel room in advance. I would pick up Jared at the airport, take him for lunch and, if I felt he was safe, he could crash at my place. If not, then I would find a hotel.

Since I hadn't told Jared about the sleeping arrangements, he would not be surprised either way. He was only staying until Sunday morning, a blessing because that meant I only had to survive forty-eight hours.

I arrived at the airport a little early. He would only have a carry-on, so I figured I would park in the garage and then meet him at the gate, avoiding the whole crazy baggage claim traffic where, like the mall, everyone forgets how to drive.

I grabbed a coffee and waited in a chair outside the gate area. Tampa airport has shuttles that carry passengers from the main airport to where I was waiting. At the designated time, I started watching the shuttles arrive.

I looked at the picture Jared sent me again, the first one, of his face. I kept scanning the crowd hoping I would recognize him, when I suddenly found myself in an embrace.

"You are more gorgeous in person," he said.

I hugged him back. "Thank you." I hoped I didn't sound as surprised as I was.

As he pulled back from the embrace, two things hit me. The first was that his amazing smile was better than his picture. The second was he didn't look like his picture. It wasn't as if he had sent me a picture of a random stranger, more like when a girl gets a glamour shot done and you can see how it is them, but it isn't at the same time. The expression on my face must have been obvious by the way his smile faded.

Whore Tip: Never send a picture of yourself that doesn't look like you, the real you. There is nothing worse than deceptive packaging.

"You're disappointed," he finally said.

"No, just surprised!" An understatement. "How was your flight?"

"I am just glad to be here, with you," he said turning on the charm. He leaned in for a kiss. I froze. Then his lips hit mine, and not knowing what to do, I gave in. This was going to be a long forty-eight hours, I thought.

He had traveled to be all this way to be here with me and I did get along with him, so I would find a way to be a trooper. I could do what was needed to get through the weekend, and then decide how to tactically withdraw.

Whore Tip: Chemistry is everything. Never forget that.

We went to a sandwich shop I knew and then to a park. I love being outside in acceptable weather in Florida, which basically means anytime when it isn't one-hundred degrees with one hundred percent humidity.

As it was a very pleasant seventy-five degrees, a picnic it was. We sat on a bench and ate. We made small talk, and he continued to be sweet the way he was on the phone. I couldn't fault him for that, but I didn't see him the same way I had before. We hung around the park for a couple of hours. I was readying myself for what was to come. I knew that when we arrived at the hotel or my house, he would want to take things to the next level, which was to be inside of me.

I decided to take him to my house. However this was going to end up, I wanted to be in the place I felt the most comfortable. He wasn't creepy or gross; he just wasn't what I had been expecting, by a long shot.

> *Whore Tip: Be careful building up partners in your mind that you have never met in person. They may end up something of your creation, instead of the person they actually are, and will never live up to your fantasy.*

When we arrived at the house he put his bags down and let me show him around the house. I left the bedroom as the last stop. From our phone conversations, he planned on ravaging me the moment we were near a bed.

I walked into the bedroom first and before I could turn he was behind me. He moved his arms around me pulling me against his body. I felt his lips against my neck, kissing and nibbling. His hands explored, trying to touch every inch of me.

"God, Randi, I want you so badly," he whispered.

I flipped the switch in my own head and imagined that I was with the Jared of my fantasy. I closed my eyes and let myself imagine everything I hoped would happen.

A moan escaped my lips and that was all the encouragement he needed. I felt his hands on the bottom edge of my shirt and then he pulled it over my head. He undid my jeans and knelt down to push them down my frame. I was wearing the black lacy thong that he had enjoyed in the photo. As he motioned for me to step out of my sandals and jeans he made sure his hands or lips were not far from my body for long.

Feeling his hands gliding up my legs, he began to rise behind me, his hands touching me as if he couldn't get close enough with just his fingertips.

I felt his warm breath against my skin just before his tongue on my thigh, then up to follow the path of my thong. With little nibbles, pulling at the thong, I heard him growl.

Whore Tip: Sounds are as important as touch and smell. Don't underestimate how much a sigh, moan or growl communicates to your playmate.

I felt his fingertips slide to the front of the thong. Gently playing with the edges of the fabric he sent shivers through me. His next growl was hungrier and his hands moved to my waist while his lips found my spine. Alternating between kisses, bites and licks he moved up to stand behind me. His fingers moved to unfasten my bra and gently removed it, kissing my shoulders and then tossing the bra to the floor.

He whispered, "I want to taste you."

"Please." I could feel how wet I was. I let him turn me around to face him. He was still fully clothed. I looked at his full lips and dark eyes, exactly as they were in the picture and I focused on them. My hands cupped his face as I press my lips against his, initiating a kiss for the first time. I pushed my tongue into his mouth, and he moaned. He pushed the kiss deeper, his teeth biting my lower lip as he walked me back to lay me on the bed.

He straddled me, unwilling to break the kiss and moved his hands to gently tug at my nipples, now hard round buds. His lips moved down my throat to my collar bone, then to my breasts. Smoothly running his tongue between my breasts, he licked around the areola of one, then sucked my nipple into his mouth. I could feel his teeth, and the pain enhanced my arousal.

He tasted down my body until he was on his knees at the edge of the bed. His fingers looped around the scant fabric that rested on my hips, the only barrier between him and the moistness of my folds.

He tugged the thong off, and then his hands moved up my calves to separate my legs, exposing all of me to him. I heard him growl again. "God, you are amazing," he said as he kissed up my thighs, savoring each movement closer to my awaiting arousal.

I felt his breath getting closer. The contrast between the warmth of him and the slight chill in the air almost made me climax. I did my best to hold myself still, even putting my hands under the pillow, to resist pulling his lips against me.

When his mouth was just inches away, my legs began to tremble. I knew I was close and wouldn't last much longer. I felt the tip of his tongue slide between my legs and then push against my clit. I climaxed, my hands shooting out to grab the blanket as I writhed in ecstasy.

He pushed his tongue in further, hungry for me, wrapping his arms around my thighs to hold me where he wanted me. It felt like he drank me in, licking and sucking. Within moments, I came again, hard, and every touch sent chills through my body. I had to push him away to let the waves of orgasms happen.

He backed away and I felt him watching me as I moved to the rolling orgasms that were taking me. I began to calm down and opened my eyes to see he had undressed. He was fully aroused and I saw it for the first time. IT WAS HUGE!

There was no way in hell that thing was fitting in any part of me. I was stunned, shocked and terrified all at once. Seriously, HUGE!

He moved towards me. I looked up, hoping that somehow my gaze would communicate that I was scared to death. From the hunger in his eyes and my juices still on his mouth, it didn't.

I didn't know what to do. Panic began to set in, the complete opposite of what I needed to have happen if he was going to attempt, which he clearly was, to stick that space shuttle inside of me.

I closed my eyes, took a breath and then in a very sexy voice said, "Jared, wait, I don't..."

He was ready for my rebuttal. I should have expected that, considering he had told me he had had this problem his entire sexually active life. "Don't worry, baby, I will be slow, you are so wet. I promise I won't let it hurt," he said.

I lay back on the bed and tried to think of anything else but being run through. He got on top of me and whispered, "I can't believe how amazing you are, how good you taste. You are my fantasy come true." I know he said those things because they were what he believed I wanted to hear.

Unfortunately, any willingness to cum again left when the beast had been released. I was trying not to clench.

He grabbed a pillow and slid it under my lower back. I let him move me the way he thought it would be best. He tried to maintain sensual movements, but I was letting it happen the way you do when you go see your gynecologist. They put you in the positions they need and you let them penetrate, while you close your eyes and try to relax.

Then it happened. I had my eyes closed and my arms lying somewhat crossed above my head. He was leaning down closer to me, in the missionary position. I felt the head. I took a deep breath, and tried to relax enough to let it happen.

When he pushed the head in, it hurt. I was being stretched the way I assume you are stretched when you give birth, but this time from the opposite direction. Medically, I'm pretty sure that is *not* a good thing.

He tried small, slow thrusts. I know he tried to be gentle, but it hurt, a lot. I was just about to tell him to stop, and I grabbed his hips and opened my eyes. That was enough for him. He came, and as he did he pushed a little deeper inside of me. I yelped in pain and he almost jumped off me pulling out.

"Are you okay?" he asked, with genuine concern.

My hands were cradling my cash-and-prizes. The pain was a throbbing ache, and I almost asked him to get me an ice pack to put on it.

"I... I... it hurts," I eventually said, after a solid minute of breathing. I just lay there for a bit as he went to the bathroom, removed the condom, (I'm still not sure where he found one his size) and got a warm wet cloth for me to clean up with.

When he brought the cloth back he attempted to be a gentleman and help, but I snatched the cloth away from him before he could touch me. Even my attempts to clean up were painful. I told him to give me a couple minutes and I went and took a hot shower. Besides needing the comfort, I needed to think.

When I finally came out of the shower he had made coffee and was sitting in the living room waiting for me.

"You're not okay, are you?" he asked with some sadness in his voice. I shook my head and carefully sat down. We talked for a bit and I told him how amazing the foreplay and the oral had been. I complimented him on what was pleasurable before I explained that there was no way in hell his cock was going anywhere near any of my orifices again... ever.

Jared looked like I had struck him in the face when I delivered the news. I didn't know how to console him on this. I let the silence sit between us until he finally said that he understood. He had been through this before, and he had hoped, because of my size, that it would work.

I was about to be offended at the comment on size, but I realized he didn't know how human anatomy works.

Whore Tip: Genitals are not based on the size of the body. A petite waif can still have a "hallway you can throw a hot dog down and watch it slide unhindered", and a six-foot-five" strapping man can have a "Tic-Tac that begs you to ask if it is in yet". Never judge the cash-and-prizes of your potential playmate by the outside packaging.

I told him I understood, then gave him the lesson on size not equaling *size*. He laughed at the hot dog reference, and made a joke that someone like that, might be, the kind of woman he was looking for.

We ended up ordering a pizza in for dinner and watching a couple of movies. Jared slept on the couch that weekend. He offered his oral service several more times, but I had to refuse. I was bruised and sore for the next week.

On Sunday, I drove him to the airport. I let him kiss me passionately one more time. As I was releasing him from what I thought was the final hug, he whispered in my ear, "I love you, Randi."

30

GAME OVER

"What the fuck just happened?" I practically screamed into the phone. I hadn't even gotten in the car to leave the airport before I called Alex.

"Um, yeah, you need to actually start from the beginning if you want me to understand anything you are talking about," Alex replied.

"Jared just dropped the 'L' word and then got on the plane," I said in a voice that was way too loud for the parking garage I was walking through. This was confirmed when several travelers walking to the bank of elevators began to stare and point.

In most circumstances, I try not to appear a complete crazy person to strangers. You never know who may be influential in your life. Right then, I didn't care. Jared had completely broken the rules.

When I turned my attention back to my phone once inside my car, Alex was laughing hysterically.

"You are presently being the opposite of help in this situation," I said, very annoyed.

"The 'L' word huh?" She began laughing again. It wasn't the sympathetic ear I was hoping for. I told her I was going to drive home, and I would call her later. She was still laughing when I hung up.

I called Lucy, and then Baley with the same result. This wasn't helping. I called Sally last. Unfortunately, Sally thought that at some point in the adventures I was having, I would find my new love. This just agitated me more.

"You guys have so much in common, he really likes you," she pleaded.

The next words out of my mouth were not ones I was proud of. "His dick is too big to fit into my pussy. I am sure that is a sign we are not a match." There was a long silence. I eventually apologized, and told Sally I would call her later.

Frustrated and pissed, I went home and spent the night trying to figure out how to get the upper hand. I wasn't even sure what the upper hand in this situation was.

Jared texted the next day and I ignored him. I ignored him for several days until he called me ten times in one day with just as many text messages. If I continued to ignore him, he would show up on my doorstep. One of the last texts he had sent me said so. I made the call.

"Hello?" he asked because even though I had called him, I wasn't speaking first. I didn't know what to say that wouldn't basically scream that I was a raging bitch.

'I'm alive, you can stop calling," I replied. Yep, in full bitch mode.

'I'm sorry, Randi. I shouldn't have told you that. I just thought... let me explain, please? I know you're mad." He was pleading.

"Fine, explain," was my reply.

Jared went on to tell me that I was everything he ever wanted in a woman, and that being down here, just being close to me was the best time in his entire life. He had never felt a connection like he did with me.

I was prepared for that part.

He continued to explain that he knew his penis was not workable for me and because he felt the way he did, he had already begun looking into penis reduction surgery to make it the perfect size for me. He told me I could choose the size, anything I wanted and that is what he would do.

"What?" I said, stunned.

"For you Randi, my love, I will make my penis exactly what you want. It only takes eight weeks of recovery. I can move down a month after. We can be together," he said. I could see him almost beaming over the phone. He really believed he had it all figured out.

> *Whore Tip: Never change yourself for another person or what you think they want. Change, especially a body modification, should only be done because you want it for you.*

"What?" I repeated.

"I want to be the man of your dreams," he said.

I shook my head. I couldn't believe this was happening. For a minute I thought it was a weird dream caused by the overall vodka consumption during the last six months, but there was no way I had drunk *that* much.

"No," I finally said after a very awkward silence.

"What?"

"No, Jared. I don't want you to reduce your cock for me. I don't want to choose a cock size. I don't want you to move down here and I don't love you." I did my best to take the aforementioned bitch out of my voice. "I am sorry. I explained to you what I was looking for. Everything you are saying right now tells me you either didn't understand or chose to ignore it. I am going to hang up now, please don't call me again."

CLICK.

> *Whore Tip: Never lead a person on. If you give them the wrong idea, it will just grow and become worse for both of you. "Being nice" can lead to stalkers.*

168

Jared did try to call, text and email me several times after that. I never replied. The worst part of the whole thing was that I had to make a new character in the game because he could find me there as well. Eventually he got the hint, three months later.

I did save the picture of his manhood in my phone. After all the dust settled, Baley pointed out that I should consider it a compliment to my sexual prowess that a man was willing to go that far to be in my tunnel of love. I gagged.

31

Cars That Go Zoom

After the horrible situation with Jared, I took a breather for a month. I needed to make sure I didn't repeat my mistakes, which meant avoiding sex with online gamers. If you play the same games they do, they can find you and they will. Then, BAM! Repeat.

> *Whore Tip: Never 'play' where you 'play'. It is like sleeping with someone from work. If you're into a sport, club or game and the playmate is not on the repeat list, it will be nothing but awkward.*

One lazy Tuesday night, I was shopping on one of my dating websites and an email popped up from TheCorvetteGod. I almost dismissed it, because it was a terrible name and instantly screamed that he was compensating for something. This was one of those moments you look back on and kick yourself for not sticking with your gut.

Instead, I looked at his profile. I was pleasantly surprised that most of his online pictures were not of the Corvette, which was a good sign. He was my height, around my age, and had black hair he kept short, in the pictures at least. He looked of average build and he had a nice smile.   Nothing jumped off the page about him other than he had a lot of similar interests to myself. I thought that something average might be nice after everything I had dealt with.

His email was short and simple, saying "Hi" and he thought I was very attractive. I call this the fishing email: short with a compliment. This is how guys usually throw out a line to a girl to see if he gets any bites.

> *Whore Tip: If you are going to be on dating sites, learn to fish. This is the most efficient use of your time. If you say hello and throw out a nice compliment and the other party is interested, they will respond. If they don't, walk away. They are not into you. Take the hint.*

I replied with the obligatory "Thank you" and something about one of the TV shows he mentioned. We ended up chatting back and forth in email. I did my normal spiel about not looking for anything serious, and he was surprised but interested.

We moved the conversation to a phone call, and agreed to meet that Friday for dinner at a restaurant that was centrally located.

During the week we chatted a couple of times via text with funny anecdotes about how our work week was going. It was nothing too serious, and it was awesome.

By the time Friday rolled around, I felt very relaxed about the date. I put on a summer dress with spaghetti straps, and a pair of strappy sandals that matched. I left my hair loose, and my makeup was just a little mascara and lip gloss. I figured since I was meeting Mr. Average, by the real name of Chad, for a light dinner at a casual spot, I would be as casual as possible while still making a good impression.

I arrived at the date not caring what happened. If it bombed, I was okay with it. If it didn't, well, even better. I felt zero pressure, which was refreshing.

He was waiting for me when I arrived and looked exactly like his picture. He smiled as I walked up, and said, "Wow! You are even prettier than your pictures!" He gave me a nice warm hug.

I hugged him back and while doing so felt that he was slightly overweight. He wore it well though, and so far things were going exactly as I had hoped. He held the door for me as we entered the restaurant. We'd chosen a steakhouse, the kind of place where they give you a bowl of peanuts and let you throw the shells on the floor.

We were seated at a booth and Chad let me choose where I wanted to sit first. As we perused the menu, he asked me what looked good. I told him I was going to get one of the house special steaks that was decked out with bacon and melty cheese. When I asked him what he was getting, I felt the first small ripple in my calm pond.

Chad revealed that he had had Lap-Band surgery just over a year prior. He could only eat small quantities at a time. He showed me with his hand how small of a portion he could eat.

> *Whore Tip: Never talk about any conditions you have on the first date. If it is something the other person has to know in order to date you, then tell them* before *the date. Otherwise, make the first date accommodate the condition so they can get to know you. Then you can be judged as a package, not as baggage.*

I suddenly felt like my eight ounce steak, salad and baked potato were going to make me look like a pig. I paused to wonder if boys ever felt that way when the girl only consumed a small salad. I took dessert off the table, which was sad, because that steakhouse had one of the most amazing chocolate molten explosions in existence.

I looked down at the bowl of peanuts, while he continued to explain why he had made the choice for the surgery after he had difficulty losing weight. He didn't see the deep breath I took.

When the waitress came over I ordered the six ounce instead of the eight, and got broccoli instead of a baked potato. I hadn't explained my meal plan, so Chad was none the wiser.

Waiting on my dinner and his snack to arrive, I asked him about his car. He spent the next twenty minutes telling me all about finding the Corvette and restoring it to the perfect condition it was in. He had done most of the work himself and it was the car he had wanted since he was a boy.

I could expound in detail all about the car, but I will sum it up: It was black, with black interior. It also had blue lights that he custom installed, so it was like you were in a spaceship, especially at night.

Ripple number two.

When the food arrived, I tried to eat quickly so that he wasn't staring at me after he finished his handful. He ate more than the size portion he had shown me with his hand, in fact almost double that. What is the etiquette on asking if someone's stomach is going to explode like something from one of the Aliens movies? I didn't bring it up.

When we finished, he asked me if I would like to come to his house for coffee. He had an arcade set-up at his house with several old school games, which happened to be some of my favorites. So, I agreed.

32

LIPSTICK TUBE

He gave me his address in case I got lost following him. I texted all the information, including his license plate number, to Sally and headed out. It was about a twenty minute drive from the restaurant into a nice, middle-class neighborhood. He had explained at dinner that he owned a two-bedroom, two-bath house and he had a dog that was part lab and part something else he didn't know. He had gotten her from the pound.

His dog was adorable and loving, and followed us around as he gave me a tour of his house. He was a huge fan of the show *LOST* and had collectables from the show, including figures of the entire cast, still in boxes on the shelves around the TV. Since I wasn't looking to date him, I didn't care what he was into.

He brought me the promised cup of coffee, with cream and sugar, and showed me the game room, the only room he had left off the previous tour of the house. When he turned on the lights, it was fantastically eighties. The entire room looked like an old arcade. It was really well done, and I admired the work he had put into it.

I sat on a stool and played a couple of games of Mrs. Pac-Man. He watched and told me about where he found the games and how he had restored some of them himself. I hoped with all this talk about building and restoring things, he was good with his hands in other areas.

He was leaning in close, watching me, when I decided to seize the opportunity and move the night along. Playing video games is fun, but I was there to play with something else. I turned my head so we were only inches apart and looked into his eyes. I gently licked my lips, then gently bit the side.

That was all the prompting Chad needed to lean down and kiss me; gently at first, then more passionately. When he finally broke away he helped me to stand and took me to the bedroom.

When we got there, he undressed me slowly, as if savoring every moment. He was still clothed when he laid me back on the bed, which had black sheets and comforter, and then turned off the main lights. A blue glow was apparent all around the top of the room.

His room matched his car.

Ripple.

I heard the sound of clothes being removed as my eyes adjusted to the new lighting. I took a breath and told myself that his kissing hadn't been horrible. I heard a drawer open and the familiar sound of a condom wrapper being opened.

> *Whore Tip: Yes, you should know what a condom wrapper being opened sounds like. You should also know what a condom feels like going in, and never believe that being on the pill is enough for either side of the encounter. People lie.*

I saw the shadow of him coming toward me just before I felt him move onto the bed. He ran his hands up the inside of my legs and spread them apart. I tried closing my eyes and giving in to the moment. I had done it with Jared, I could do it now, I thought.

I felt his tongue begin to lick my folds. Unfortunately, it was the same as I'd imagine his cute dog lapped up water. It was rough, and there was too much pressure. His technique turned painful and I had to move to get him to stop.

How did I do this? Smack him on the head? Clamp my legs closed on his face? No. I simply said the magic words, "I need you inside me."

Those words always work on a person who is not really interested in pleasing you first, and is instead doing what they need to so they can move on to the part where they get pleasure.

Whore Tip: You know you are a good lover if giving pleasure is as enjoyable as receiving pleasure.

He climbed on top of me and pushed my legs apart to accommodate the missionary position. I felt something and then he began rhythmically moving back and forth as if he was fucking me. I felt nothing. Was he priming for penetration? Was he pushing in just the tip? Was it *in* yet? I had no idea what was happening. I know women who joked about being with a guy with a small penis, but it had never happened to me.

I lay there, Chad moaning and grunting, sounding like he was enjoying himself. I wondered if this was what a guy feels like when he sleeps with a girl whose vagina is so large it's like pounding a mayonnaise jar. That thought was all I needed to lose the mood.

I grabbed Chad's shoulders as he continued to thrust at me, and told him I wanted to see him cum on my breasts. I told him to turn on the lights and let me see him explode all over me.

I didn't want any of those things. What I wanted was to stop whatever this was and see what kind of machinery he had down there.

The tactic worked and he turned on a lamp next to the bed. When my eyes adjusted to the light I found him standing over me, stroking himself.

He was using his thumb, index and middle finger on the smallest penis I had ever seen in real life. He came on my chest, and I did everything I could not to stare at his tiny cock. It was shaped like a tube of lipstick and about the same size in length and girth.

Talk about the opposite of my last encounter. I actually felt sorry for him.

He went to the bathroom and grabbed a wet washcloth and a towel. I took the offered items, but excused myself, saying I needed to use the ladies room.

I cleaned myself off, went to the bathroom and stared in the mirror. That wasn't a good idea. The more I thought about the little situation I had gotten myself into, the more I wanted to laugh.

I stifled my giggles, washed my hands and took a steadying breath as I walked back in the room. He was laying on his side and patted the bed next to him. I tried to think on my feet, so I told him it was getting late and that I needed to get up in the morning. He patted the bed again and asked me to stay for just a little longer.

I should have grabbed my clothes and gotten dressed in the car on my way home. Sometimes, I'm too nice. Maybe it was the sympathy I felt for his lack of manhood, but either way, I lay on the bed with my back to him, thinking it would be safest.

He put his arm around my waist and pulled me closer, kissing my shoulders. He whispered, "This is nice," and snuggled his head against mine.

Just when I thought it couldn't get any worse, a horrible smell assaulted my nose. I looked down to see if the dog was in the room. No dog.

A gigantic rock had landed in my calm pond, way beyond a ripple.

When the first wave of smell finally seemed to abate, another one, even worse than the first, assaulted my nose. An involuntary gag escaped from my lips. Chad sat up and I followed suit.

I grabbed my clothes and went into the bathroom. After dressing I came out to find him in the living room in a pair of boxers and a T-shirt.

"I am sorry. Because of the surgery, I can have pretty bad gas sometimes, especially when I am relaxed," he said sheepishly.

I simply nodded.

What are you supposed to say to someone who is horrible at oral sex, has a tiny dick and very bad gas?

"I have to run. It was interesting meeting you, Chad. Goodnight," I said. I grabbed my purse and left. He had begun to get up to walk me out, get a hug, or something. It didn't matter. I wasn't waiting around to find out what further surprises TheCorvetteGod had in store for me.

On the drive home, a part of me felt a little bad. The following days with Chad texting and calling made me feel worse. It is a horrible feeling, when you are put in a position where you can't say what you think without potentially destroying another person's confidence.

I told Chad that I didn't really think we were looking for the same things.

It was a lame excuse, but it was the only one I could come up with. He stopped calling after that.

33

THE SUIT THAT MAKES THE MAN

J ust when you think that life has become a satisfying adventure, you find yourself in the middle of a tar pit. I can imagine how dinosaurs felt. It's a terrible thing to experience.

If my recent adventures had taught me anything, it was these two gems:

Shopping for the right playmate can take time;

My wall between emotional connection and physical connection was firmly in place.

The latter was proven to me one night when the ex decided to rear his head.

The girls and I were preparing to go out dancing. The night was to be dedicated to just the girls. I had promised to keep my "milkshake" in check, and have fun out dancing without any boys.

It was about ten pm and all the girls were at my house putting the finishing touches on the evening's attire and make-up, when the doorbell rang. At first I was afraid I had made plans with BI, or someone else, and forgot.

I rushed to the door and peeked out the window. "Shit," I said out loud to no one in particular.

Alex was in the hallway and asked, "Who is it?" I was standing with my back to the door, leaning over, the position I had resorted to upon seeing who my visitor was.

I scrunched my face and whispered, "It's Allan."

"Are you kidding me?" Alex said, not whispering. The doorbell rang again.

I knew it was going to end badly. It had been almost a year since I had come face to face with the cheating heartbreaker. I was a little surprised that my immediate reaction was annoyance rather than being upset.

Alex started for the door, just as Sally and Baley poked their heads around the corner.

I turned and opened the door before Alex could. Looking back, it might have been entertaining watching her handle the situation, but I thought I could be blunt and he would just leave. Of course, I am not that lucky.

As I swung the door open, he turned. Allan was my height, had brown hair that he kept short, and had blue eyes. He had a nicely muscular build and he was wearing a suit. For the record, he never wore suits. I didn't even think he had ever owned one.

"Hey, gorgeous," he said with a smile.

I rolled my eyes. "What do you want?" I asked, hoping that I sounded as pissed off as I felt. He was making me angry just being there. All it took was opening the door and seeing him, acting as if he had any right to do that.

"Aren't you going to let me in?" he asked as he pushed his way past me into the house. He didn't physically move me, but I didn't want any bodily contact, so I had no choice but to move.

"Oh look, it's an asshole in a suit," Alex said, crossing her arms.

Allan ignored her and turned to face me. "Can we talk?" he asked me.

"Now?" I asked, dumbfounded.

"Yes. I got this for you." He waved to his suit. "I've changed. I need to show you."

All I could think was, "Is this really happening?" Then I simply blurted it out.

"Baby..." he started.

"Don't 'Baby' me. Why are you here?" I said. My face was flushed. When I had dreamed about this I had hoped that I would remain calm and icy cold. Instead he was heating me up, and not in the good way.

"Randi, honey, you know I am the one... the one to make you cum," he said as he started to move toward me. He reached out his hands to cup my face. I think he was going to try to kiss me.

I was done. "Get the fuck out, Allan. The only thing you can make me do is junk-punch you if you don't leave in the next ten seconds."

He looked flustered. Did he seriously think that, by buying a suit and laying on the charm, I would swoon? I wanted to vomit.

I held the door open and just stood there until he walked out. He turned on the porch to say something, but I slammed the door and didn't hear it.

He showed up at the club that night and tried to talk to me again. It only took a few words to my favorite bartender to get him escorted out of the club. It was amazing how satisfying it was to watch him have a second door slammed in his face in one night.

34

HELLO, MRS. ROBINSON

On almost a daily basis I was getting the "Are you into younger guys?" messages on the various sites that I shopped on. Every now and then, I was tempted to give it another try. Since Richard (Brief Intermission) was so much fun, I figured there were more potential students out there waiting to be taught how to please me.

> *Whore Tip: Learning what is pleasurable is not a one size fits all kind of instruction. There are some basic guidelines, but every lover is different. Remember, you can never stop learning more about what your current playmate likes and doesn't. Don't think you know it all. You don't.*

I met Nicolas one night. He was honest in saying he was in college and had only ever kissed one girl before. Nick told me he was very shy, and didn't want to look like an idiot when he finally got up the nerve to ask a girl he liked out.

He told me that that wasn't some cheesy pick-up line, and he was a blank slate if I was willing to teach him.

I told him I needed to think about it. I asked him to give me a week and promised to let him know what I decided.

My first thought was that I wasn't into charity cases. The other part of me thought that I might find a true diamond in the rough.

Nick was twenty. He was five-foot-nine, so shorter than me. He had blond hair that was buzzed close on the sides and longer on the top. You could see his shyness in his online photos, and his profile was sparse at best.

When I showed his profile to Lucy and Alex, they both commented that it must have taken a lot of courage for him to even ask me what he did. I had to agree. It was a big step for him.

Whore Tip: Beware that there is a high percentage of people online who are working an angle and are not what they appear to be. Be sure you don't decide everyone is working it, because you will blow off the good ones.

Exactly one week later, I told him I would help him out if I could. He asked me where I would want to teach him. He lived in a dorm with a roommate and I didn't want him to know where I lived. Although he seemed sweet and innocent, stalker and creepy can happen really quickly.

I told him we were not going to have sex before I assessed his potential, and we should meet down by the beach. It was public, but at night there was privacy, and since I figured we were only going to first base, it was a safe choice.

He agreed, and we agreed to meet a couple nights later. I made sure I picked a spot where I could park and walk up to the meeting spot. I wore jeans, a tank top and flip-flops. It was going to be a working session and I wanted to be comfortable.

He was wearing shorts and a polo shirt. He had watched me approach and was fidgeting the entire time. I thought he might explode from nervousness when I walked up and said, "Hello, Nick?"

"Hi... Hello. You're Randi, right?" he said, stammering.

This was adorable. "Yes, that would be me," I said, smiling. "Take a deep breath, Nick, or you might pass out before we ever get started."

He did. He took a deep breath and then launched into a long string of thank-yous for my willingness to help him out.

I told him that we had yet to see if I could be of any help, but I was willing to give it my college try. This made him laugh a little. I stuck out my hand for him to take, as we walked towards the beach.

When we got to a good spot, I asked him to show me his ID. This threw him off, but he complied. I needed to make sure he was of legal age; he looked like he was seventeen in person.

> *Whore Tip: It doesn't matter what age a playmate tells you they are, it matters what age they actually are. Being labeled a sexual predator because you took someone's word for it is beyond stupid.*

After we sat down, I asked him what it was he wanted to learn. His response was that he wanted to learn everything. I told him I wasn't qualified to teach him *everything*, but he didn't get the humor.

I told him to relax; it would never work if he was nervous and tense. We took a couple of deep breaths together, and I asked him to tell me about school and hobbies, what kinds of girls he found attractive, that sort of thing. Eventually he relaxed enough for me to give it a shot.

"Kiss me," I said in a whisper, and leaned in a little, closing my eyes. I needed an assessment of what I was working with.

It took him a moment, but he eventually pushed his lips against mine. It wasn't an actual kiss, more like he just pushed his mouth into mine. I pulled back. He was not a natural at all.

I explained a little of what kissing was about, the motions, how to meet someone's lips then I leaned in and kissed him. When I pulled back, he was pitching a tent in his shorts.

He hadn't kissed me back, at all. As a matter of fact, he hadn't really responded. I hadn't even introduced the concept of the tongue yet.

I sighed. "Nick, listen, you have to move when you are kissing someone." I showed him my lips moving, at first just by themselves and then against my hand. I curled it into the kind of puppet mouth you would make as a kid.

He nodded and said he understood.

I said, "Okay, let's try this again."

And I did, over and over again. I worked with him for almost two straight hours. I even let him touch my breasts, on the outside of my clothes. He hadn't earned second base, but I thought it might jar loose whatever wedge was holding his sexual door shut. I was wrong.

In the end, I kissed him goodnight, on the cheek, and left.

As I was driving back, I checked in with Sally to let her know I was still alive as I did after all my encounters. I called instead of texting, because I felt as if I had run a marathon, uphill, in the snow, during an avalanche. I was exhausted.

Sally told me that one of the first boys she had ever kissed suffered from a very similar situation where his mouth didn't seem to work. She had put more time into her project because it had been a junior high boyfriend, and she really liked him. That was understandable. If you are twelve you may still have a chance.

Nick texted me later that night thanking me for my lesson. He went on to tell me that he looked forward to future sessions and that he had been really turned on.

I replied: "You're welcome."

When he asked me to help him the following week, I sent him a rejection letter. I wished him luck but my class was too advanced for him and he needed to find a tutor before re-applying.

Whore Tip: There is a difference between being nice and being a crazy person giving your time to something that will never be worth the effort.

35

THE "NEW GUY"

I needed a change of pace. I wasn't ready to give up on my adventures, but it seemed I had hit a rough patch.

I became a lot pickier as I shopped. There was no end to the stream of willing men wanting to come out and play with me, but I had struck out three in a row. One night, Baley came over and I went so far as to write a bizarre question list for the potential playmates to answer. I tried to phrase the questions to seem casual, but they were more like interview questions. I might have become a little paranoid, but I really needed to have some fun, and asking a bunch of veiled questions was fun, which was the point after all.

After passing on several candidates, I met Ronnie. He was six-foot-four, brown hair, hazel eyes and a slightly crooked smile. He lived in Sarasota, which was about an hour south of me. The drive seemed like it might be a deal-breaker, but he told me he didn't mind the drive. He had also answered every one of my ridiculous questions perfectly. I was impressed.

I was also happy that when he asked why I had such a silly list of things I wanted to know, like "How important was his car to him?", he laughed and told me that he had a few questions for me as well. Interesting.

He wanted me to tell him about my best and worst encounters. I was honest. The best so far had been Todd; besides the cheating part, of course. The worst was The Pilot, sexually speaking. I could have said Jared, but I didn't really get to know what that was like, because he didn't fit. Ronnie thought the whole thing, including my sometimes brutal honesty, was amazing.

He was twenty-seven and in college studying to be a lawyer. He worked as a waiter at night in a fancy restaurant near his house. With such a full schedule, I was surprised when he said he would drive up on Saturday night after his shift.

I told him my friends and I were going dancing and he thought that was a perfect opportunity. He wouldn't get to my neck of the woods until almost one am and this way I wouldn't be waiting up for him. We would also be in a public place and if we didn't click he had simply taken a really long road trip.

That night, I had to remind myself not to drink too much. Sally, as usual, was our driver for the night. I think I've mentioned that her being allergic to alcohol has its perks for the rest of us.

We arrived at the club around eleven pm. There was no point in arriving any earlier because the place is usually deserted until later anyway. We had our first round of shots, on the house from my favorite flirty bartender, and headed for the dance floor.

At midnight, I checked my phone. Ronnie had texted at eleven-twenty-eight pm that he had gotten off a little early and was on his way. I texted back: "Meet you on the dance floor 😊". The text seemed cute and funny, but that may have been the vodka.

I let the girls know he was on his way. It wasn't often they got to see more than pictures of my playmates, so they were excited, too. This could end up being awkward for Ronnie, but he had been warned and had agreed with full disclosure from me.

I checked my phone to see if he replied and he had. "I'll be the guy showing you my moves, so watch out."

I replied: "I'm terrified now."

He sent back: "😊". This was going to be fun, I could tell.

It was about thirty minutes later that I was on the dance floor with Alex, Sally and Baley when I felt a hand go around my waist and I was pulled back against a frame larger than mine. I heard him say, "I hope you're Randi, otherwise this is how the Irish say hello." This made me grin and I turned to see his cute crooked smile.

I reached up and wrapped my arms around his shoulders. "This is actually how the Irish say hello," and I kissed him. He kissed me back, circling his arms around my waist. I found my new favorite way of saying hello.

> *Whore Tip: Be yourself always. If you want to be spontaneous- DO IT. What is the worst that can happen? Now imagine the best that can happen... See why it's worth the risk?*

The girls had stopped dancing when he had come up behind me. Alex was looking at him like she would punch him in the face if I didn't respond well. I love her protective nature.

It took a couple of minutes for me to stop kissing Ronnie. Besides the fact that he was a great kisser, he smelled amazing and was gorgeous. JACKPOT!

I introduced him to the girls. They were all excited for me and he offered to buy a round of drinks for all of us. I gave him our order and he was off.

"He is so hot," Baley said when he walked away. We all watched him, which wouldn't have been weird if we hadn't been standing in the middle of the dance floor. We made our way over to a high top table and waited for our next round to arrive.

When Ronnie got back he handed each girl a shot, except Sally, who had a coke with an umbrella in it. He told her it was because her drink needed to be perked up a bit, which made her smile. He was charming.

*Whore Tip: Being charming and playful will always
score points with people you want to score with.*

We spent time talking, laughing and dancing. Ronnie was
incredibly easygoing and funny. He made it comfortable to just
casually hang out.

We were dancing close together, my back to his front, pressing
against each other, moving to the beat. I could feel his cock grow
and press against the black dress pants he wore. He had left right
from work and was still wearing part of his uniform.

He moved my hair away from my neck, pulling it onto my opposite shoulder and began kissing and biting at my neck. If we had not
been in public, I would have jumped him right there. It only took a
moment for me to decide we should leave, and soon.

I told him, "I needed to say goodnight to the girls."

He looked almost confused for a couple of seconds, and then
a smile crept across his lips. "Yeah, I should say goodnight to
them, too."

I walked over to the girls and let them know we were going to
head out and Ronnie was going to give me a ride home. In front of
him, I gave Sally all his information. He actually gave her his phone
number before I could look it up in my phone. With all of the good-
byes out of the way, we headed out of the club and back to my house.
We couldn't get there fast enough.

Fifteen minutes later and my keys were in the door as quickly
as possible. I barely had time to shut the door before he was pulling
my top over my head and moving me towards the couch.

His lips found mine, and I couldn't get his clothes off fast
enough. As we feverishly threw each other's clothes to the ground,
I felt my core tingling. Just touching him, feeling him touch me,
had me on the edge.

He pulled back and asked, "Condoms?" It was just one word
but I wasn't sure what he was asking, so I paused. "Sorry, I meant

do you have some, I didn't bring any and well..." he said, answering the question on my face.

I smiled. "Be right back," I said and went into the bed room.

Whore Tip: Always be prepared. Like an adult equivalent of the Boy Scouts.

When I returned, wearing nothing but a smile, I held a couple of options in my hand for him to choose from. Before he made his selection, he matched my lack of wardrobe. He walked up and pulled the condoms out of my hand while using his other hand to pull me against him, taking my mouth with his again. His tongue sliding against mine, I nibbled on his lower lip and he growled a little.

He surprised me by wrapping his other arm around me, picking me up and carrying me over to the couch before setting me down. He stepped back and made his condom selection, letting the rest fall to the ground. He slid the winner over his very hard cock.

Getting a good look at his long, thick shaft for the first time was mesmerizing. He was above average in both length and girth, but in a very appetizing way.

He looked at me and smiled. "Well my sex kitten, how do you want me?"

I scrunched my face a little, pretending to contemplate the options. I already knew exactly what I wanted. I pointed at the couch and told him, "Sit."

He complied willingly and I walked up to stand before him. He ran his hands up the outside of my thighs, my hips, my waist, to my breasts and took one in each hand. "Wow, these are amazing," he said smiling.

"Thanks, I like them," I replied.

I put my right foot beside his leg and then my left on the other side. He looked slightly perplexed and then I lowered myself down and grabbed a hold of his raging hard-on, sliding it inside of me as I moved against him.

I held onto the back edge of the couch and began to move myself up and down his length, plunging him deeper and deeper inside of me. He moved his arms underneath so that he cupped my ass and could use his strength to move me faster.

My moans got louder the faster we moved together. I came once, then again. I could feel him getting closer, feel him growing harder as groans escaped his lips. I looked into his eyes as I leaned back, giving into the motion, the sensation of him filling me completely as I climaxed again. Just then his fingers dug into my hips, pulling me down hard against him as I felt his release.

My legs felt weak and my arms were the only thing holding me in place as I leaned back up to meet his lips. After a kiss and continued heavy breathing, I moved to lay on the couch. His head was back and he ran his fingertips along my legs, now across his lap. We both were quiet for a time, simply enjoying ourselves.

Without much conversation, it wasn't long until we were both sound asleep in my bed. In the morning, I woke to see him pulling on his boxers and heading towards the bathroom. I got out of bed, pulled my hair into a messy bun and put on PJ bottoms and a cami top.

> *Whore Tip: Just because you are at their house or they are at yours doesn't mean you are required to have a sleepover. If you're not feeling it, you can always call a taxi.*

He joined me in the kitchen as I was making coffee. I excused myself to use the facilities and take a look at how my make-up had fared from the night before. It was not a pretty sight. I grabbed a make-up wipe and made myself as presentable as possible.

When I returned to the kitchen, he had poured us both a cup and I grabbed the needed cream and sugar. We simply sat and drank the warm, caffeinated goodness. After a few minutes, he started smirking.

I hoped it wasn't because I looked like a spooked raccoon with circles of eyeliner and mascara. I thought I had remedied that with the wipes.

I took another sip and attempted to look cute.

"You're fun," he said, smiling and taking another sip, his eyes never leaving mine.

"You are pretty *fun* yourself," I said mimicking him.

"Do you think I could convince you to head down my way?" he asked, using what I am sure he thought was his charming voice. It was.

"Possibly," I replied with a wink.

We finished our coffee, he got dressed and we had one last amazing kiss before he headed home.

36

HEADING 'HIS' WAY

I t was a little over a week before Ronnie texted me. One of the items we had discussed was that for it to be a casual relationship you couldn't require constant communication. It had to be just that casual and it couldn't have too many requirements.

I was at the mall with Sally doing what we called a "movie montage". It basically consisted of going clothes shopping, but trying on anything that caught our eyes. For Sally, it always included fancy dresses and hats.

If I told you how many clothes my amazingly adorable friend Sally has in her closet because of these shopping excursions, Paris Hilton might become jealous.

This texting session between dressing rooms went like this:

Ronnie: "Hello Beautiful"

Me: "Hiya Sexy"

Ronnie: "Up to anything fun tonight?"

Me: "Always, but I can be persuaded to change my plans 😳"

Ronnie: "Is that so?"

Me: "With the right temptation"

Ronnie: "How about you come play at my house tonight?"

Me: "Tempting..."

Ronnie: "How tempting?"

Me: "Very!"

Ronnie: "I'll consider that a yes."

Me: "Deal. Text me your address and a time to arrive."

Ronnie texted me his address and that he got off work around midnight depending on his tables. Because he was a waiter he would have to wait for his tables to leave and then do his side work before he could head out. He said he would leave his door unlocked so I could let myself in. He would be there as soon as he could.

Whore Tip: Finding a playmate that makes things simple can be even more fun than the adventurous ones. It means more pleasure and less work.

It turned out it was almost a two-hour drive to get to where Ronnie lived. I was thankful I looked it up on my GPS before I left the mall parking lot. I had of course, given Sally the details. I had not driven that far away for one of my adventures, but she felt a little better knowing she had met and liked him.

Sally insisted I wear my school girl outfit to see him. She said since he would have been working a long, hard day, he deserved a treat. I knew the reaction I got from most men when I wore that outfit and I agreed. I would be in for a treat, or two, myself.

As I was about to head out around ten pm, I texted Ronnie to let him know. He texted back: "Be prepared for a shower scene".

I replied: "Like in Psycho?"

"Maybe 😳".

I had already counted on staying the night, and, not wanting a repeat of raccoon eyes, I kept my make-up simple. Light eyeliner, mascara, both waterproof, and twenty-four-hour lipstick. None of it was going anywhere without a good scrubbing.

It was a little difficult to find his apartment when I got to his complex. Each set of six buildings was in a circular pattern, with water fountains and artistic brick walkways, and what appeared to be no numbering.

After a couple of missteps, I finally found the right apartment, and since none of the neighbors called the police, I guess I didn't scream criminal. I'm pretty sure anyone who did see me in my knee-high white socks, plaid miniskirt and super-tight white button-down top thought call girl instead. I was fine with that.

I opened the door to his apartment. It was on the top of three stories and had vaulted ceilings. There was a small kitchen which had a bar with stools, and a small dining area that had a desk, books and a ton of papers, which I assumed was his office. The living room had a long brown couch with many cushions, a coffee table and a huge TV.

Ronnie had told me he was a sports fan. Although I enjoyed watching sports live, I really don't get into watching it on TV, with the exception of hockey.

I opened a door off the living room to a huge master bedroom. It had a king size bed against one wall that had a TV built into the headboard. I wasn't sure how one watched TV at that angle, but I knew there had to be male logic involved in its placement. I closed the door without the need to invade his privacy further and went back to the couch, placing my backpack on the ground.

> *Whore Tip: Snooping around another person's place, home or office, is tacky. Plus, if they are only a play-mate you may find out more than you ever needed to know. Would you want them snooping around your world?*

I had brought my purse, a change of clothes, some condoms and a toothbrush. All this I put in a backpack. If you are going in a costume, you should make sure you accessorize properly. I never do anything unless it is one-hundred percent.

I texted Ronnie that I was at his place and then tried to figure out the remotes. I know most people reading this would think I must be dumb that I couldn't figure out how to turn the TV on, but with four remotes and none of them labeled...? I tried a few buttons, got the TV to turn on, but wasn't able to figure out how to get to the cable box input setting. After a few minutes of frustration, I turned everything off.

On the coffee table were what looked like four piles of blocks. Upon closer inspection I saw they were puzzles. I lay on my stomach on the couch, knees bent, propped on my elbows like a high-schooler and tried to figure them out. I wasn't sure how much time had passed when I heard the door open and turned to see Ronnie dressed very similarly to how I met him the first night, but this time with a tie. He had the same amazing smile.

Whore Tip: A playmate dressing a certain way to please you means just as much as you doing it for them. Make sure to let them know what turns you on.

Ronnie walked over towards me as I got up from the couch. He stopped suddenly, drinking me in with his eyes. He mouthed "WOW", as he gestured for me to turn around. I turned slowly so he could take all of it in. When I stopped, I stood in a coy pose to look a little shy. I play the part well.

He walked up slowly, a smoldering look in his eyes. It was as if he wanted to devour me right there. Without a word, his lips met mine. The kiss was intense, his tongue pushing my lips apart with need, and I responded in kind, biting his tongue and lips a little.

He bent me back a little, and I wrapped my arms around his neck. I trusted him not to drop me. To my surprise he wrapped his other arm around my legs picked me up, and carried me into his room and then the bathroom.

37

Hot, Steamy and Wet

He didn't stop kissing me until he set me down on the long counter in his bathroom. He was smiling again as he pulled back and turned on the water in his shower, which was separate from the tub.

The shower was square, tiled from top to bottom with grey slate. It had a glass shower door with an opening at the very top to let steam escape.

I was sitting facing him, my knees bent and legs spread apart. My skirt rested on the top of my thighs, and I placed my hands behind me on the countertop. This pushed the front of my shirt open just a little more.

He began to remove his clothes, watching me. He removed his tie first, then as he undid the buttons on his shirt I bit my lower lip. When he let the shirt, fall to the floor, I felt my panties become wet, and not from the steam.

Shirtless, he walked up and pushed my legs farther apart, running his hands up my thighs. I let my head fall back as he kissed my neck, down my throat, following the opening of my shirt.

I had worn my red lace bra and boy-shorts to match the plaid skirt, and both were peeking out from underneath the clothes that attempted to cover them up. He bent down to remove my shoes and slowly pulled off each of the socks, kissing and licking down my calves as he did. As much as I wanted to close my eyes to enjoy the sensations of heat and the wetness of the steam billowing all around, the warmth of his mouth, his lips and his tongue on my skin, I couldn't stop looking into his eyes.

When he removed the last sock he stood up and began to unbutton my shirt. I moved to undo his belt and pants and let them fall to the floor.

He pulled me to my feet then, and turned me around so I was facing the mirror, shirt open. As I stood there with the foggy image of him standing behind me smiling, I heard him whisper, "You are my fantasy." He kissed my neck as he pulled the shirt from my shoulders.

As he dropped it and his fingers worked to unzip the skirt, my hands went to the counter. I felt the warmth spreading from my core. I was so close, I bit my lip again as a moan tried to escape. The skirt landed around my ankles.

Next he unhooked my bra. He used his fingertips to push the straps off my shoulders. I felt my legs get weak and goose bumps erupt across my skin. He was perfectly deliberate with each motion, using his fingers and his lips to tease me.

He pushed himself against me. I could feel how hard he was even with his boxers and my boy-shorts still between us. His hands moved from my hips to slide up my waist to my breasts. His fingertips explored until he had each of my nipples between his fingers. He tugged on each nipple right as he bit the nape of my neck. I climaxed. My hands grasped at the countertop, trying to keep myself from falling as the waves of pleasure hit me.

He pulled away from me and his hands went to the last remaining clothing on my body. As he moved them down my legs, I could feel his breath against my skin. I was trembling as he stood, having removed his clothing as well.

Leaning close to my ear, his skin against mine, he breathed, "Wanna get wet?"

"Too late," I said, as I turned to smile up at him and brought his lips to mine.

> *Whore Tip: Never underestimate the orgasmic power of foreplay. Penetration with proper lead up is like winning the sex lottery!*

I entered the shower and let the warm water wash down my body. I turned to see why Ronnie hadn't joined me yet, when the shower door opened. It was like a scene from a movie. The steam billowed out the shower door as he entered.

He had taken the time to ensure he was properly protected for round two. The look in his eyes was pure lust. In one smooth motion, he closed the door and pushed me up against the back wall of the shower. The tile was cool against my skin and my back arched slightly as his lips met mine. I wrapped my arms around his shoulders to pull him closer. I couldn't get enough.

Ronnie lifted my right leg up to his hip, and grabbing his hard cock, he slid it inside of me. Having already climaxed, I was tight. The force of his penetration came with a pressure and slight pain that made me gasp and dig my nails into his back as I took all of him.

He lifted my other leg so I had to wrap both my legs around his hips, while his hands went beneath my bottom for support.

I rode his motions, and, for every thrust of his, I pushed back against him, trusting him, every moment filled with ecstasy. It wasn't long before I was squeezing his ever-growing cock. He brought me to the edge and pushed me over so many times I lost count. My screams mixed with his moans and growls as he got closer, until in one final, deep thrust that filled all of me, he erupted.

38

WORTH THE TRIP

After the shower, we lay on his bed and watched a movie. It was late, and we both fell asleep a couple of times trying to stay awake.

At some point, Ronnie woke me up by sliding his fingers inside of me. This turned into me straddling his face as I took his throbbing manhood into my mouth until we both came again, fully spent.

We woke up the next day, after sleeping in 'til almost noon. We had sex in the bed for the first time, and even missionary was fantastically orgasmic with Ronnie.

We decided to go out to breakfast around two pm. We ate waffles and drank coffee at a cute local diner that was Ronnie's favorite. We talked about a hundred different topics, but not a single one was about our real lives or what this thing we were doing was. It was perfectly simple.

Ronnie became a regular playmate. Every few weeks, one of us would make the drive, and every time it was worth it.

He was one excuse the girls never minded I use to end one of our nights out early. They knew my night with "The New Guy" would end with me smiling and spent. My time with him also allowed me to be comfortable with playing again. He reminded me that what I was looking for was out there for the taking.

39

What's in a Number?

Late one night when checking my email on one of my shopping sites I received a message from RockStarSeven. The name didn't impress me, but I had learned that online names are not usually well thought out.

Mine was usually AmazonGoddess, but not everyone is as clever as I am. When you pick names like AnalLover27 or ISuckToes21, it is kind of a giveaway what you may be into. This method works to weed out anyone not into your sexual preferences, before they even see your profile. Others don't think their name all the way through and sound simply desperate, like WomanLover867 or LonelyGentleman1979.

Do not give away too much personal information in your name. With current technology, it doesn't take much to find you on the internet, or for a person with less than good intentions to suddenly make your life uncomfortable, or worse.

For goodness sake, don't use TampaAmy1983 or MarkfromLargo1979. That reveals your name and age, and, for someone with enough patience, a search is easy enough to accomplish.

Lastly, it is important for those out there in the dating market to realize that the name on your dating profile is the first impression someone has of you. As the old commercial said, "You never get a second chance to make a first impression." So make a good one.

Mr. RockStarSeven's email was:

Hello AmazonGoddess,

Everything about your profile seems too good to be true. I am sitting here hoping it is and that you will give me the chance to meet a Goddess in person.

— Seven

Of course this was flattering, any remotely intelligent person on a dating site will start with a compliment. After looking at his profile I was a little intrigued. Seven, if that was his real name, was a drummer in a heavy metal band.

He had tattoos on his arms, legs and head, which he kept mostly shaved with the exception of very long, naturally red hair that started just under his hairline and fell to his shoulder blades. He had a hoop piercing through the middle of his lower lip.

He was a ginger rocker and surprisingly attractive. I read his profile and saw we had almost nothing in common besides enjoying playing video games in our free time. That was even a stretch, because his choice of games wasn't even close to mine.

> *Whore Tip: Sometimes the best lovers are the kind you have literally nothing in common with. That way there is zero chance you would slip and decide somehow they are dating material.*

I replied with a quick "Thank You" and asked what the name of his band was. He replied almost instantly, and we began to talk. I didn't bother asking him why he had emailed me when I didn't seem like his type. From my pictures, he thought he saw something he liked. The trick was to see if any attraction still held true in person.

He seemed funny and smart in the email conversation we had that night. I did finally ask him if his name was actually Seven. Turns out it was his stage name and what all his friends called him. I didn't ask what his real name was. For what I potentially wanted, his stage name would work perfectly.

He asked me when I wanted to meet up, and said I could come out and see his band play at a bar the next weekend. I said I would think about it.

I looked up the band he was in. It was not quite heavy metal, more a mix between hard rock, punk and hair band, at least from the sound of the few recordings I found and his lead singer were concerned.

The venue they were playing at was about forty minutes north of me, so I brought up the idea to the girls to see if this interested them. It did.

I let Seven know I would be there. I also let him know that I was going with friends and he would need to find me in the crowd. He accepted the challenge and promised a round of drinks for me and my friends.

We arrived at The Bourbon Room in a small town north of Tampa. The venue boasted not only music, but two nights a week they hosted MMA fights. As we pulled in, Lucy started to get a little panicky.

The parking lot, which consisted mostly of dirt and gravel, was in front of a strip mall that hosted the venue, a pawnshop, and a gun store. Most of the parked cars indicated a certain, shall we say, level of income different from ours.

I think what pushed her over the edge was the crowd that was milling around outside. Aside from the obvious biker gang, most of the fans looked like burnouts. I had to smirk a little. "It's an adventure, Lucy, just don't give out your real name," I said, and got out of the car.

We had all decided to dress the part for what we thought a punk/metal fan would look like in the most stereotypical ideal we could imagine. Alex and I were wearing corsets with jeans and boots. Lucy and Baley had chosen more of a goth look, wearing all black and darker make-up. We fit right in when we walked through the doors of the smoke-filled room.

There were five pool tables to the left, a long bar and some tables to the right. Straight ahead was a stage and the band in the process of setting up. Several heads turned when we walked in. The music being piped in was loud and we headed over to the bar where I ordered the first round.

As we took our drinks, we looked towards the stage to see if we could get a glimpse of the drummer. Sure enough, we were not disappointed. He came out carrying his cymbals to finish setting up his kit. He was very focused on the task, which gave me, and the girls, the opportunity to size him up.

He was wearing a black T-shirt with some writing on it, black lace-up boots that almost reached his knees and a black kilt. This surprised all of us. Conversation turned to whether or not he was wearing anything under his kilt. I told the girls that I could find out right then if they wanted me to. Alex shook her head and ordered another round. Party pooper.

After about fifteen minutes, the band started to play. We moved closer to the stage, and enjoyed the show. They played for about an hour. Some of the songs were good and catchy, others were not as practiced as they could have been, but it was fun overall.

It was also fun fending off some of the guys that approached us, some with manners and others without. Alex ended up elbowing one of the suitors in the chest. Under most circumstances, that would get you removed from a bar; instead his friend bought her a drink.

At one point during their set, I made eye contact with Seven. He had looked up on a break, sweat pouring down him. A drummer is the most physically intensive member of a band and it showed, on that small stage in a room that wasn't cooled enough for the number of bodies.

He looked out into the crowd. I think he was scanning to find me. Our eyes met, he smiled, and I winked.

When the lead singer, who had spiked hair with pink tips, announced their final song I was a bit relieved. The novelty of the night had started to wear off and I was ready to go.

The final song was a crowd favorite called "Punk Rock Girl". It was the best of the songs they had played and when they took their final bow the applause was loud. Seven had taken one of his drumsticks and thrown it into the crowd, the other he pointed in my direction and tossed to me.

> *Whore Tip: Never let the apparent fame or actual fame of a person lead you to think it will make them a better lover. It will end badly for both of you if they are on a pedestal of what kind of sexual encounter you think they will be.*

The band left the stage and we made our way back to the bar to have a final drink and settle our tabs. During the performance, I had decided that if Seven and I were going to play, it wasn't going to be that night. Whatever he had to do to break down after the performance, I wasn't willing to wait around for. I was willing to meet face to face and see if it would lead to seeing him again.

We drank the final drink and watched some of the best drunken games of pool we had ever seen, when I felt someone tap me on the shoulder. I turned. He was as cute as his pictures, with very light green eyes.

He smiled. "Thank you for coming."

I smiled back. "Thank you for inviting me." I introduced him to the girls and he shook their hands.

He asked me if I was going to be hanging out for a bit and I told him that we were going to head out. He wanted to buy us the promised round, so I let him. We talked for a few minutes, before some of his band mates came up to him to tell him he needed to clear his gear from the stage.

I told him not to worry and to let me know another time he was free so we could meet up. He agreed and started to move in for a hug. I held my hand up before he could make contact and said, "Rain check?" gesturing to his very sweaty condition. He smiled and nodded, and gave me a kiss on the cheek instead. He had nice full lips, but the piercing was cold when it made contact. I couldn't help but think it would be a weird sensation on other parts of my body.

I left, willing to give him a try. I was curious to see if being with a guy in a band was as wild as it was professed to be.

40

CAN A DRUMMER BE OFF KEY?

I didn't meet up with Seven for a couple of weeks. He had gigs and I had other playmates on the schedule. When we finally connected up, he asked me out for breakfast and if I wanted to come over to his place after.

We met up at a diner near his apartment. I wore a plain white T-shirt and shorts; he was in shorts and a T-shirt with a metal band's logo on it. I asked him about being a drummer. He described his entire musical career from when he started playing, his first band, the first time he went on tour with a band and how he ended up in his current band.

It took up the conversation time for the entire meal. I knew two things when he asked me if I wanted to go to his place to see his drum set. The first being that I could only see doing this, or him, one time. Unless he surprised me and was mind blowing in bed, I knew we would have a hard time with even idle conversation. Second, I wanted to know what that piercing would feel like on my clit. I told him I would follow him home.

His apartment was exactly the way I pictured it. He had a female roommate, because being a drummer didn't pay enough to live on his own. I was going to ask him what he did for a living to support himself between gigs, but it quickly became apparent that there was nothing he did between gigs.

He showed me his drums, which took up most of the living room. Then he showed me his room. It was surprisingly clean. There was a full size bed, band posters on the wall and a small computer table in one corner.

When he finished with the mini-tour he came up and wrapped his arms around me and pulled me close to him. He leaned in to kiss me, but before his lips hit mine he whispered, "You are so sexy. I have been thinking about kissing you since I first saw your picture."

He started gently kissing me at first, and then more aggressively. I was ready to be ravaged like a groupie.

He walked me back towards the bed, his lips never leaving mine, and laid me down. His hands were touching me on the outside of my clothes, feeling my hips and breasts and squeezing my ass.

His grip was hard and I moaned. I wanted more. I wanted him to rip my clothes off and toss them so that when we were done we would have to hunt for where my bra ended up. I was ready.

He pulled back from kissing me and looked down, scanning my face for a minute. "What?" I whispered, trying to sound as sultry as possible, but wondering why we had suddenly stopped.

"Do you like to be kinky?" he asked grinning.

"Depends, what do you have in mind?" I asked. It always makes me nervous when a guy asks that. There are plenty of kinky things I am more than willing to do, but a few are reserved for a trusted playmate.

His face started to get a little red.

"Can I play with your feet?" he asked.

I have had this request before. I know different parts of the body turn people on. I don't mind having my feet and toes sucked and licked as long as the person doesn't go "foot to mouth" and try to kiss me after.

I nodded.

He asked me to lie on my stomach, then got up and moved to stand at the end of the bed. He pulled at my feet to move them closer, so my knees were on the edge of the bed. When I turned to look back at him he asked me to face forward. I complied, but the "Ravaged by a Rock Star" fantasy I had was fading.

I brought my arms forward, so I could lay my forehead against them. Listening, I heard him unzip his pants and then the sound of them hitting the floor. Next, I heard the sound of a plastic cap. I felt his hands lift my right foot and begin to massage it with what I assumed was lotion.

It felt good and I began to relax a little. I enjoyed the feeling of his fingers as they put pressure in my arch and between my toes. He moved to my left foot. I lay there and wondered if this fetish was his foreplay. That's when he brought my feet together and I felt something thicker than a finger slide between them.

Everything in my brain screamed to turn around and see what the hell was happening, but I knew. He was fucking my feet.

Holding them together, he slid his cock in and out of the very lubricated opening he had made between my arches.

His rhythm quickened and I heard moans escape his lips. Weirdly, I felt him grow thicker as he got closer. I held my calves as firm as I could, so he could move my feet the way he needed in order to climax.

Then it happened. His grip tightened and he exploded all over the bed and the back of my legs. I shook my head, closed my eyes, and let my legs fall when he let them go.

"Don't move," he said, and he left the room. I lay there hoping that his aim had been good and the globs of his man goo I was feeling on the back of my thighs hadn't landed anywhere else on my person.

Whore Tip: Be responsible when you are coming on your playmate. Make sure they are ready, willing and

able to take the blast. Getting spooge in certain places,
like an eye, can be painful.

Normally, causing my lover to have an orgasm was a moment of pleasure and pride mixed together. I couldn't name the correct emotion for feeling like a blow-up doll. Blow-up dolls don't usually have very good feet though, I thought.

He returned to the room, and I still didn't move. He used a somewhat-warm washcloth to clean up the mess he made on me and the bed, and only after he was done did I move.

I got up and put my flip-flops back on. Grabbing my keys and phone, I met his gaze. I could tell he was confused. I simply tilted my head and said, "This was fun," and headed for the front door.

As I was reaching out to grab the door knob, the door swung open. A woman, who I assumed was his roommate stood before me. She seemed surprised, and asked "Who the hell are you?"

I smiled and said, "A foot model" as I moved past her toward my car.

Seven tried to call me several times after I made my escape. I never answered. I went home and took a long hot shower. I finally understood that scene in the *Crying Game.*

41

LAWN CARE GIANT

S ometimes you meet a giant when you least expect it. I was in a local building supply franchise shopping for light bulbs and filters for my house when I heard a deep voice behind me. "Need help finding anything?"

I began to turn around and answer "No, I think..." Before I could finish my sentence I was rendered speechless. Standing before me was a towering giant. At least six and a half feet tall, possibly taller, he had deep brown eyes and dimples, which were on full display as he smiled. His shoulders were wide, and standing just feet away from him, I felt tiny.

I stood there, holding onto my filters, and realized my mouth was open in awe. I snapped it shut when he asked, "Are you okay?"

I cleared my throat and nodded. "Yep, good. I'm good."

I wasn't good; I was acting like a total idiot. He continued to stand there and smile at me. He seemed to be waiting for me to do or say something, anything. I looked down to his name tag. Mark.

"Well, Mark," I started, "How do you feel your knowledge level is in the light bulb department?" I looked at him quizzically, while I tried to regain some of my composure.

"Well..." he said, and paused. It took me a second to realize he was waiting on my name.

"Randi," I said.

"Well, Randi, I have the most experience in lawn and garden, but sometimes people use lights in their backyard, so I will endeavor to help you in any way I can with your light bulb purchase." He gestured in the direction of the light bulbs.

After several minutes of witty small talk about the merits of different bulbs and which is right for each kind of lamp, I made my selection.

I could tell Mark was a little disappointed our encounter was about to be over, when he asked if I needed to pick up anything else on that fine Saturday. I shook my head and thanked him for his help.

He smiled again and told me he would be here if I ever had another light bulb shortage. I smiled and began to turn away. Taking a chance, I turned back and asked, "Are you any good at light bulb installation? It is a very dangerous undertaking and I could always use some support." He laughed louder than I think he expected. Several customers turned to see what was causing all the racket.

He regained his composure and took out a small pad from the apron he was wearing, wrote something on a sheet, tore it off and handed it to me. I grabbed the paper, turned and made my way to the checkout.

I didn't look at the paper until I was in my car. It said, "I get off at eight tonight. Meet me at House of Beer at nine-thirty pm."

I called Sally to give her all the details I could. She wasn't pleased, but I told her I wouldn't go anywhere with him without more information. Reluctantly, she agreed to my plan.

That night, I arrived at the House of Beer, a local bar and brewery. Mark was sitting at the bar, a beer half-finished in front of him when I saddled up on the stool next to him. Even sitting, he towered over me.

I wore a simple sundress, strappy sandals with a three-inch heel, and my hair up in a ponytail. Mark was now in jeans and a polo shirt, and it turned out he was six feet eight inches tall. He told me it had been my height that drew him to me in the store. That, and how nice my ass had looked in the shorts I had been wearing.

We chatted over a couple of beers. When he asked about me, I decided to be very blunt. I usually didn't have this conversation in person. I found myself blushing a little while I explained what I was looking for, that I didn't want to date anyone and that meant I didn't want to know too much about his personal life or have him to know too much about mine.

He took another drink from his beer and looked at me. He might have been waiting for me to say that I was kidding. Instead, he said he was impressed with my honesty, and that I wasn't like any woman he had ever met.

Having the conversation took all of the tension out of his posture. He ordered a third round and wanted to know if he could ask me some questions about my playmates. I was an open book on that subject, I told him. He laughed at that and asked me several questions; the first ones were tame, but then he moved into detailed questions about my sexual desires.

> *Whore Tip: There is something to be said for a person who knows exactly what they want and goes for it. Never limit your actions in favor of what you think another wants. Be honest and be yourself. It is so much more fun that way.*

By the end of the third beer, I knew Mark was eager to play with me and we elected to head to his place. Before we left, he gave me his address and phone number just in case I lost him when I followed him home.

When I got in the car, I texted everything to Sally, whose only comment was that I must emit a pheromone of some kind because boys were drawn to me like a magnet. I told her that if I could I would bottle it, sell it and be a millionaire.

42

You must be this TALL ——- to ride this RIDE

Mark's house was a three bedroom, and had a very open floor plan. I walked into an ideal bachelor pad. The entire place was laid out for the comfort of a single guy, including a pool table and bar in the back room, a TV that took up an entire wall in the living room, and a huge U-shaped leather couch.

The décor was mostly done in black and white, and he had large saltwater fish tanks with colorful fish in almost every room.

I didn't waste any time when he showed me his bedroom. The bed was the largest I had ever seen. It was a California king, he told me. Because of his size, he had considered ordering a custom bed, but this way he could still find sheets.

I walked towards the bed, taking off my shoes, then my dress, and then my undergarments. When I crawled onto the bed and turned to face him, I was wearing nothing but a smile. The look in his eyes was that of a hunter stalking his prey.

I knelt and placed my hands between my legs on the bed. I waited for him to make his move.

He began to pull his clothes off and move towards the bed. As his pants hit the floor and he pulled off his boxers, I was surprised. I don't know what I was expecting. I knew better than most that the size of a man doesn't dictate the size of his manhood. The difference in proportions between Mark and "little Marky" was alarming.

He was hard; I could see it standing at attention between his legs, but something was off. Before I could put my finger on it, he had moved to kneel on the bed. Even matching my stance, he still had to lean down to kiss me.

His kisses started out soft and sensual. As he became more intense, the kisses got a lot sloppier. I had to pull back several times and maneuver his lips to my neck or ear to avoid him sucking in my entire face.

He moved me back to lay me on the bed and when I saw him loom over me I shifted my position so that I was on top. I was afraid that we wouldn't connect without some well thought-out maneuvers.

It was easy enough to change the direction of this encounter by whispering into his ear, "I want to ride you". He smiled and lay back, which let me straddle him. *If* I could straddle him. There was a problem. The width of his hips was dramatically larger than mine. When I tried to squat over him like I had with Ronnie on the couch, I could not get a stable stance.

This was becoming awkward.

I decided to kneel between his knees until I came up with a strategy to climb this 'mountain' of a problem. As I ran my fingers down his chest, his stomach, and then to his thighs, I was able to get a good look at his equipment. Besides not having put on a condom, he was not very well endowed. He was not small, but definitely below average. This, coupled with his body size, made the situation Mission Impossible.

> *Whore Tip: Don't hurt yourself trying to make something happen. If it isn't going to happen, then use your escape plan.*

He looked down at me and I did the only thing I could think of: I started stroking his cock with one hand and running my fingernails over his skin with the other. I am sure he thought I was doing it as foreplay, but I took him all the way home, letting him explode all over himself as he climaxed.

I got off the bed, headed to the bathroom, washed my hands and brought a towel back to clean him off.

He was still lying on the bed when I left. I told him it was later than I thought and I had to be up in the morning. He smiled and said he couldn't wait to hear from me for our next play date. I told him that I wouldn't hold my breath on that one. He laughed. Sometimes honesty is so brutal that people have to file it in the humor category to deal with it.

I had to find another home store to get supplies from, which was inconvenient. This is why you should never play in a place where you may need to visit again. I was happy I had never done anything with my sexy bartender.

> *Whore Tip: Never lead someone on; if you're not interested, tell them. If they don't believe you, it isn't your job to convince them. Being nice will only lead to more drama. Nip it in the bud before it starts.*

43

JESSIE'S GIRL

I was tired of ending up in the bedroom with prospective play-mates only to find out they were not qualified to be on the team. These catastrophes had to end. I had to start testing the waters before jumping into the pool again.

I was thrilled when the next man who appeared in my life was like something out of a steamy romance novel.

Alex and I had gone down to the beach to a club located in one of the hotels that had a "sink or swim". Sink or swim is where you buy a cup at the door for twenty dollars, and drink all you want, all night long. Anytime we participate in one of these it means a lot of sinking and very little swimming.

> *Whore Tip: Make sure when you are on the prowl and you are drinking that you bring backup. You never want to wake up and chew your own arm off to get away.*

We had taken a taxi, because we knew we were not going to be in any condition to drive ourselves home. We had the taxi service programmed into our phones and were prepared for a night of fun.

Alex and I had been dancing when she told me she was going to the restroom. I know it seems like female bathroom etiquette that

I should go with her, and I hate to break it to you, but not all girls fall into that stereotype. Considering what happened next, I was very glad that I had let Alex venture to the ladies' room by herself.

I loved the song that was playing and I was moving my body to the beat, hips moving side to side. I had closed my eyes and was in my own little world when I felt a hand move around my hips. I opened my eyes to find the sexiest man I had ever seen in real life moving against me. He was six feet two inches tall, had blond hair cut short, blue eyes and muscles for miles. He was dressed in jeans and a white tank shirt tight enough for me to see his six-pack.

I looked up into his blue eyes and licked my lips. He was yummy! I was feeling nice and toasty from the drinks we had been consuming from the aforementioned cup, so any shyness at this amazing piece of man meat in front of me had vanished.

> *Whore Tip: Although drinking can let down some inhibitions, you should never use it as a crutch. It isn't who you are, and being yourself is sexier than being a drunk. I promise.*

I danced with him for several songs. Letting him lead me, moving in perfect rhythm to his movements, melding my body with his, I was lost in everything that was the man in front of me.

I ran my hands down his arms and chest, touching as much of him as I could, bringing my mouth within an inch of his, only to lean back and let him pull me to him. It was amazing.

A little voice tickled in my head and I realized I didn't know where Alex was. Breaking the spell of him the next time he turned me so I had my back to his chest I scanned the room. I saw Alex sitting at the bar with a very attractive man with black hair, in a button-down top. We made eye contact and she tipped her glass in my direction. She was fine and I was in heaven.

I heard him speak for the first time. "Is that a friend of yours?" he said into my ear. I nodded and he turned me to face him. "What is your name?" he asked.

"What is yours?" I replied. This caused him to smirk.

"I asked you first," he replied.

I licked my lips, looked him up and down before leaning into him. "Do you always get what you want?"

"Always," he said.

"So do I." I pulled away and walked to the bar.

As I ordered a drink, he walked up and put his arm around my waist.

"Where do you think you are going?" he asked.

I looked back at him and asked, "Thirsty?" He chuckled and nodded. I told the bartender to make it two and turned to face him while we waited for our drinks.

"Are you going to tell me your name?" he asked again, resting his hands on each side of my waist. I shook my head slowly. "Playing hard to get?" he asked with a devilish look in his eye. I shook my head again.

It might have been that I was more than a little drunk, but it made me a lot bolder and it was incredibly fun.

The bartender arrived with the drinks and I turned to put a tip on the bar. When I turned around again he had walked away. I scanned the room to see he was talking with Alex down the bar. He nodded in my direction and she whispered something to him. He said something else to her and headed back to me.

"Randi?" he said, as he took the drink I held out to him.

"Clever," I said, as I took a sip of my drink.

"Want to know where my friends are so you can ask them my name?" he said teasingly. I simply shook my head again and walked out to the dance floor.

He followed and we danced, enjoying the feel of each other. Alex came up to me with her new friend to let me know she was going for a walk on the beach. I nodded and leaned in to my dance partner to tell him we were going for a walk on the beach. He looked a little confused until I nodded toward Alex and her new friend's direction. He grabbed my hand and we followed them out.

Walking on a beach when you are intoxicated inevitably leads to sitting on the beach watching the waves. Alex was having fun with her new friend, and, giving them some distance, I finally found out the name of mine. His name was Jesse.

I didn't ask him. I think it drove him a little crazy. I could tell he wanted and liked control. I would only give him a little, and then take it away.

> *Whore Tip: When flirting, the trick is to play the game of cat and mouse, taking turns being the cat and then the mouse. If you always make the move, you don't give your partner a chance to assert themselves. Make the game fifty-fifty and you will always come out the victor.*

Behind us were the lights from hotels and condos that lined the beach. In front of us was the night sky and the waves crawling up the shore and back out again. It was like being on a cusp between two worlds.

"So, Jessie," I started. "What is it that you want?"

He smiled with a smolder in his eyes. "I thought that was obvious, Randi. I want you," he said and leaned into kiss me.

His mouth was warm and strong. He put his hand on the back of my head to bring me closer to him, running his fingers through my hair and pulling a little. This was all it took and I found myself sitting on his lap, my legs on each side of his. Each kiss was more passionate and hungry then the last.

The sound of people talking pulled me out of my haze. I looked around and saw people walking towards us, chatting, reminding me that we were in public. Though part of me didn't care, I knew this wasn't the place.

I looked over at Alex who met my gaze across the beach. I knew she was thinking the same thing, time to take our play time indoors.

> *Whore Tip: Playing in public can be naughty. It can also lead to arrest and incarceration, if only for a night. Neither of those things are remotely sexy.*

I looked at the man I was straddling and asked if he wanted to come home and play with me before this encounter got an R-rating. His response was to slide his tongue into my mouth, and pull me against him so I could feel his very hard cock. I took this as a yes.

We all headed back to the club and out to where the taxis were waiting. Besides giving the driver the address to my house, there wasn't much talking. Alex was crashing in my spare room. As there were four of us, Alex and her new friend, Jessie and I, in the cab I assumed that the plan was still the same, with a couple of additions.

We arrived at my place and Alex's new friend, who had a heavy French accent, paid for the cab and we all went inside. As soon as the front door was closed and locked, I grabbed Jessie's hand and led him to the bedroom.

We barely got the door closed before he was pulling my clothes off of me. It seemed like it was only seconds and we were entwined together on the bed.

His body was perfect. I kissed, licked, and touched every inch of him. I couldn't get enough. The salt on his skin, his musk, they were intoxicating.

Just as I was about to take him in my mouth, he stopped me. He moved me so I was beneath him and held my hands above my head. Sliding down my body, he slowly kissed down my neck and my chest. His hands moved to take each of my breasts in his grasp as he sucked and pulled on each nipple. My back arched as the sensations vibrated through my body.

He continued to suck and nibble on my nipple while his fingers found my clit, wet and waiting. Gentle at first, he moved his fingers back and forth, increasing the pressure until I burst. My hands were grasping the pillows beneath my head, my back arching as he slid his fingers inside me. He stroked in and out, sliding as deep as he could push himself. I screamed out when he brought me to climax again.

Still writhing in ecstasy, he slid between my legs and I felt his hot breath just as his tongue licked up the length of my folds, drinking me in. Each motion sent shivers through me. My legs began to tremble, it was more than I could take when he sucked at my clit, and I climaxed again.

Every place he touched me sent fire through my veins. He moved away from me while I tried to regain my breath.

My mind reeling, I didn't know how long he was away, when I felt his hands on me spreading my legs. He slid between them, pushing them to my chest with his hands, and then I felt him slide inside of me.

Gentle at first, and then harder, he thrust deeper inside of me. I brought my hands to his hips, pulling him into me with every thrust. I could hear his moans matching mine as we both climaxed together.

Lying there, we took time to steady our breathing. He finally got up and went to the restroom to remove and dispose of the condom, which I was happy he had put on. I hadn't been in any condition to pay attention to that vital detail. When he returned, I took my turn in the facilities. When I came back he was under the covers. He held them up and beckoned me to join him.

It took only minutes of snuggling against his warmth to fall into a deep sleep. When we woke up the next day, we did a repeat of the night before.

When we finally left the bedroom, we grabbed a cup of coffee and found Alex sitting at the dining room table. Apparently her playmate was still asleep in the other room.

As we drank our coffee, Jesse explained that he traveled a lot. It turned out Jesse was a soldier for hire. He had been in the marines for a term and had learned that he was pretty good at what he did. Because of his job, he would be gone for months at a time with little or no contact stateside. This hadn't worked for many of his relationships, but I couldn't help but think how perfect this was for me.

When we parted ways that day it was only for a couple of hours. Jesse couldn't get enough of me, and–trust me–I wasn't complaining. We played around for the next couple of days. On a break from an especially amazing shower scene, he asked me what I was looking for.

I realized I was comfortable with where I was. I told him I wasn't looking for anything serious and that I had playmates. I waited to see his reaction. He smiled and asked if they were boyfriends and whether they knew about each other. I had to laugh.

He wondered if I would be willing to add him to my list. I told him that he would always be on top of my list when he was in town. With that he tackled me and I enjoyed a blissful evening being Jesse's Girl.

Whore Tip: When you find someone awesome who truly 'gets' you, don't let them go.

44

WHAT A GIRL WANTS

Adding Jessie to my list of active playmates, which included "Brief Intermission" aka Richard and "The New Guy" aka Ronnie, I had a full dance card.

I found that you don't have to have someone, or many some-ones, tell you that they love you. Being wanted, desired, and even worshipped does just fine.

I didn't close my shopping accounts, but I did stop checking my emails. My pantry was full.

My friends were happy that I had settled on a standard roster. They didn't have to worry so much about my extracurricular activities.

This also left me with a lot more time to figure out what I really wanted. Having the freedom to play and the awesome playmates who, each in their own way, made me feel wanted and desired, gave me the ability to close the door on my broken heart.

> *Whore Tip: Always be true to your life choices and remember the friends and playmates that support you are more valuable then gold. What is the saying? Haters gonna hate, so be the Whore you can be and NEVER change who you are!*

I was happy living on Whore Island. What is life without a little adventure?

MORE TO COME!

Slumming It On Slut Street
(Book 2 of the Randi Michaels Novels)

Visit Dalia's website:
www.DaliaLance.com
and follow her blog to make sure you
never miss another Whore Tip!

ABOUT THE AUTHOR

So here is something about little ole me; I have had a very interesting upbringing, starting with growing up in Hollywood, CA. Never shy, I learned that if you are not willing to try something new, you may let life simply pass you by. I love meeting people from all walks of life and these experiences inspire me on a daily basis. As a true friend once pointed out "You are never a complete waste, you can always be used as a bad example." So, what's the worst that can happen?

www.DaliaLance.com
Twitter: @DaliaLance
Facebook.com/authordalialance

IMPORTANT NOTE

Please take a moment to leave a review of

My Home on Whore Island!

Feel free to contact the author, too. She's kind of a big deal and

loves to hear from her fans.

Discover more at
4HorsemenPublications.com

10% off using HORSEMEN10